Libby studied him with a brooding look

"I know you're trying to be gallant here, Holden. But we have to face facts. I was the one who wanted to kiss you that night, Holden. Not the other way around."

Noting the raw vulnerability in her expression, Holden felt his heart go out to her all over again.

He realized it was his turn to be honest. No matter how much it complicated their lives. "You're wrong about that, Libby," he told her hoarsely.

His gaze lingered over her, as he paused to let his words sink in. "I would have given everything I had that night, to see where that burst of physical attraction would lead."

Dear Reader,

We all feel loyalty. To the people we love, our family and friends, the jobs we cherish and the causes and passions we pursue. But what happens when the cost of our single-minded dedication becomes too much? When it begins to feel like a negative, rather than a positive, force in our lives?

Libby Lowell loved her late husband, Percy, and his family. Now the sole survivor to the family legacy, she has been carrying on in their stead, running the three-generations-old ranch equipment dealership, living in the house where all the Lowells were raised. And last but not least, tolerating—if not exactly appreciating—the continued protectiveness of her late husband's best friend, the ever-so-gallant Holden McCabe.

Holden McCabe loved Percy, too. More, he feels responsible for the unexpected end of Percy's young life. Holden has tried to make up for that by keeping the promise he made to Percy shortly before Percy died. It hasn't been easy. Libby Lowell would rather Holden just stay away from her.

Now, both Libby and Holden are at a crossroads. Libby wants to move on with her life, have a career of her own choosing, and the family she yearns for. Holden wants to be relieved of his guilt. The only way that will happen is if Libby gets the attentive husband and baby she has always wanted, and deserves.

Holden has some ideas about that, of course. Libby isn't so sure… Together, they find the path to happiness anyway.

Happy reading!

Cathy Gillen Thacker

A Cowboy to Marry

CATHY GILLEN THACKER

TORONTO NEW YORK LONDON
AMSTERDAM PARIS SYDNEY HAMBURG
STOCKHOLM ATHENS TOKYO MILAN MADRID
PRAGUE WARSAW BUDAPEST AUCKLAND

Recycling programs
for this product may
not exist in your area.

ISBN-13: 978-0-373-75378-9

A COWBOY TO MARRY

www.Harlequin.com

Printed in U.S.A.

Chapter One

Libby Lowell had just ducked into a deserted corner of the Laramie Community Center to check her BlackBerry when a shadow loomed over her. It was Holden McCabe, as big and broad-shouldered and chivalrous as ever....

Libby frowned at the good-looking man who had been her late husband's best friend, wishing, as always, that the six-foot-three rancher did not feel so compelled to watch over her.

Ignoring the way his shirt brought out the cobalt-blue depths of his eyes, she smiled tersely. "If you're here for what I *think* you are, Holden, I have to warn you...I am *not* in the mood."

His smile full of mischief, Holden inclined his head toward the buffet tables on the other side of the crowded venue. "For pumpkin or pecan pie?"

Libby rolled her eyes and leaned in a tad closer. The truth was, she was stuffed to the gills from the delicious holiday meal. All she really wanted now was a nice long nap. "For any well-meant but totally unsolicited advice," she corrected. The kind that Holden thought Percy would have given her, and hence, intended to deliver in her late husband's stead.

Holden rubbed a hand across his chiseled jaw and continued to play dumb. "Why would you think I want to tell you what to do?" he asked.

"Maybe because just about everyone else has at some point or other today." Libby lifted a lecturing finger before he could interrupt. "And don't pretend you don't know what I'm talking about, because I saw you talking to my employees, earlier, as well as at least a half-dozen area ranchers."

He shrugged his shoulders amiably, then folded his arms in front of him. The motion drew her eyes to the solid, muscular contours of his chest.

Swallowing, she turned her attention to his ruggedly attractive face.

Libby didn't know what was wrong with her. She had known this man for years now. And yet…

Holden leaned toward her. "Of course I was chatting with everyone. It's Thanksgiving." And this year, everyone was eschewing private family gatherings to attend a holiday fundraiser for the local children's home, an event Libby had helped organize.

Not about to have her suspicions blown off, Libby lifted an eyebrow in challenge. "Really? Because it didn't look like any of you were discussing the probable outcome of the upcoming University of Texas and A and M football game." Which was what all the men would normally be talking about. She paused again and looked straight into his mesmerizing eyes. "Admit it, Holden. Everyone is coming to you. Trying to enlist your help."

Keeping his gaze locked with hers, the handsome meddler flashed a dimpled smile. "People are concerned."

"Well, they shouldn't be," she snapped.

Holden leaned in even closer and murmured, "The fear is you are acting rashly…."

"And unwisely?" she couldn't help but add.

Frown lines bracketed his sensual lips. "Because of the holidays."

Thanksgiving, Christmas and New Year's had been hard in the two years since Percy had died. Made even worse by the fact she had no other family left, on either side.

It was just her and the ranch-equipment dealership she had inherited from the Lowells. Stuck in a place that reminded her of all she had lost and would never have again. At least if she stayed in the small but thriving West Texas town of Laramie.

Which was why she had finally come to her senses and decided to stop delaying the inevitable and move on with her life, once and for all. No matter how hard it was going to be initially, she had to do it.

Ignoring the softness of Holden's gaze, Libby scrolled through the text messages on her BlackBerry until she found the one she wanted. It was from Jeff Johnston and said, Tomorrow evening at seven-thirty all right?

Libby typed in: Perfect. Meet me at the dealership. We'll go to dinner from there.

Aware of Holden reading over her shoulder, she flashed him another insincere smile, turned off her phone and slipped it back into the pocket of her black cashmere blazer.

"You're really going to pursue this?" His low, sexy voice rang with disbelief.

Was she? When just agreeing to meet with Jeff Johnston made her feel extremely disloyal? Libby pretended a cool she couldn't begin to really feel. "This is my decision, Holden."

It didn't matter what Percy or his family would have wanted, she reminded herself purposefully. None of them were here any longer....

Holden clamped a gentle hand around her elbow, the action sending ribbons of sensation flowing beneath her skin. "No one is saying otherwise."

Libby stepped back, pushing aside the sudden onslaught of sexual feeling. For years, she had been devoid of physical yearning. Only to have it all come rushing back now, with the aching desire to be touched, held…loved.

Which was something else that could not happen in this small town, where everyone still saw her as the late Percy Lowell's wife.

Fighting off her increasing feelings of disloyalty, she said, "They just want me to keep everything status quo."

"They want you to be happy," Holden corrected, looking as if he and he alone had the solution to that, too. "We all do."

Libby looked at him stubbornly, aware of the restlessness inside her. She was thirty-two now, and overwhelmed with the sense that life was passing her by. How would she feel at thirty-four, thirty-five, if she didn't act…?

"Then forget how you and everyone else feels. And give me room to pursue a possible agreement with Jeff Johnston in my own time and in my own way."

"I KNOW WHAT YOU'RE thinking, Holden, but Libby is not your responsibility."

He turned to Libby's best friend, Paige. The pediatric surgeon, and wife of his cousin Kurt, had made her way to Holden's side the minute Libby stormed off in a huff.

Not wanting their conversation to be overheard, he ducked into the empty storeroom where the banquet tables were usually stored. "I promised Percy I'd look after her and make sure no one took advantage of her," he reminded Paige.

"And you have—for over two years now. But Libby is a grown woman, fully capable of making her own decisions."

"In certain regards," he conceded. In others, she was still way too giving—and unconsciously sexy—for her own good.

Paige lifted a brow in quiet dissent.

Which prodded Holden to argue, "I don't have to remind you how emotional and overwrought she was after Percy's death." So deliriously "happy" she was practically walking on air one moment then completely devastated the next....

The look on Paige's face told him she recalled the same tumultuous swings in Libby's moods. "That was grief and hormones."

And guilt on his part. Terrible, haunting guilt.

"Beyond all that..." Paige paused. "She made a mistake—an understandable one."

One, Holden acknowledged painfully, that he and Libby had recklessly gone on to make even worse, and were both still trying to get over.

But Paige didn't know about that. And hopefully never would.

He scowled. "The point is, none of it would have happened had Percy been alive."

Libby wouldn't have trusted him with her secrets and thrown herself joyously into his arms...or called him just hours later, sobbing hysterically, begging him to take her to the emergency room. Only to find out that the terrible malady she'd thought she was experiencing didn't exist after all.

It had been a horrible, embarrassing mess. One they still hadn't figured out how to handle.

Oblivious to the complicated nature of his thoughts,

Paige sighed. "You're right. If Percy had been here, she probably wouldn't have gone off the deep end like that."

And, Holden thought, he would not have been the one to take a distraught Libby home from the hospital in the wee hours of the morning, or been pressed into staying until dawn until Paige was finally off duty and could be with her….

Paige continued with the matter-of-factness of a physician. "The point is, that time has passed. Libby's pulled herself together and made a success of the family business she inherited from the Lowells."

"To the point," Kurt McCabe stated as he strolled up to them, "that a rival businessman wants to purchase it."

Not surprisingly, the gravity of the situation had the rest of Holden's family joining them, too.

"And that," his brother Hank interjected with the expertise of a cattle rancher, "could spell trouble for all of us."

"Or not," Holden's other brother, Jeb, concluded, with the ease of a man used to taking life as it came. "From what I understand, there's nothing thus far to indicate Jeff Johnston is a shyster."

"And nothing that tells us he is not," their dad, Shane McCabe, warned in a brisk, businesslike tone. "The only thing we do know for certain is that we all need heavy farm equipment to run our ranches. And if anything happens to the tractor dealership here, we'll have to go a hundred miles to get sales or service."

"That would definitely be a pain," Holden's brother-in-law, Dylan Reeves, said, "but I think we can all agree it's not the main worry for any of us."

Holden's mother nodded emphatically. "Our main concern is Libby," Greta said with feeling. "None of us want to see her hurt. And, sad to say, the sale of the Lowell family business could be a lot more devastating to her than she thinks."

AT THE BEHEST OF HIS FAMILY, Holden decided to give it one more try. Unfortunately, by the time he emerged from the storeroom, Libby had already left for home. Holden stopped by the dessert table, picked up some sweets to go and drove to the Lowell residence on the edge of town.

The magnificent two-story stone-and-cedar farmhouse was located just across the road from the tractor dealership. Surrounded by a white picket fence and a beautifully landscaped yard, it had been in the Lowell family for three generations. Libby's Range Rover was parked in front of the detached garage. Holden parked his pickup beside it.

He was just getting out, foil-covered plate in hand, when a third vehicle drove up. The compact sedan contained two women—Miss Mim, the retired town librarian, and the twentysomething college grad, Rosa Moncrief, who had taken over from her.

So much for spending time with Libby and getting to the heart of whatever was bothering her, Holden thought.

"I am so glad you're here!" The older woman hurried forward to give Holden a hug, while the younger one shyly said hello. "We need all the help we can get."

Help for what? Holden wondered, as Libby stepped out onto the porch, looking more exquisitely beautiful than ever. She had already changed out of her party clothes into boot-cut jeans, suede moccasins and a fitted flannel shirt that made the most of her slender five-foot-five frame. Her silky, honey-blond hair had been swept up into a ponytail. She had a pair of sexy reading glasses on her face, a thick novel in her hand. As always when he was near her like this, Holden found it difficult to turn his gaze away or stifle the protective feelings welling up inside him.

Part of it was because he had made a promise to protect her. The other part wasn't quite so gallant....

Oblivious to the depth of his interest in her, Libby looked curiously from one to the other. "What's going on?"

"A bit of a conundrum." Her colorful earrings jangling, Miss Mim rushed forward to hug Libby, too. "I hope you don't mind—we asked Holden to join us."

Libby flashed him a look that said she did not exactly share the elder woman's sentiment, but smiled and beckoned everyone inside.

Holden set the plate of desserts on the hall console while Libby took their jackets. "Now, tell me what's gotten you so upset," she urged, as she led them into the sweeping living room, with its mix of comfortable modern furniture and priceless antiques.

Miss Rosa gulped. "You know we've had problems with the water lines in the library all year. Well, yesterday morning we had another leak, and Rowdy Whitcombe had to come out and start pulling up the floor. This time, he wasn't able to fix it, and he left with everything still torn up." She sighed. "Naturally, I called the county to find out what in the world was going on. All they would tell me was that a few others were coming to assess the problem and that I should get everyone out and keep the facility closed until further notice."

"That sounds...ominous," Libby murmured, trading concerned glances with Holden.

Wishing he was sitting close enough to give her hand a squeeze, he nodded back.

"Which is why I got involved," Miss Mim confided with

an unhappy sigh. "But by then the government offices had closed for the Thanksgiving holiday."

Clasping his hands between his knees, Holden leaned forward. "Did you try talking to Rowdy?"

Miss Mim nodded. "He wasn't at liberty to reveal much at this juncture, but said that if the situation was what he suspected, the library might be closed for a good long while."

"Which would be a problem," Libby said worriedly. "So many residents depend on it."

Holden knew she spent a lot of time there, too. Books had always been of great comfort to her. Even more so after Percy died….

"Plus—" Miss Rosa's low voice quavered "—we have all those Christmas events planned for the children, starting Monday. All the book clubs in the area have signed up to use the space for their holiday parties. Not to mention all the free literacy tutoring that goes on there." She wrung her hands in distress. "I'd arranged for a tree and everything!"

"And we all know," Holden murmured, "how bureaucracy can slow things down."

"No kidding!" Miss Mim turned back to Libby, her gaze intent. "We're going to need a real crusader. Which is, of course, why we came to you!"

Libby smiled. "I'll do everything I can to help."

"Me, too," Holden promised.

Beaming, Miss Mim and Miss Rosa stood. "With a Lowell and a McCabe on the job, how can we go wrong?" the older lady joked.

Holden went with Libby to show them out. "Actually, you'll have a lot of McCabes," he promised, "as soon as I let the family know what's going on."

Briefly, Libby's expression looked pinched. "As far as the Lowells go, it's just me. But I promise you I'll give the situation my all."

Thanks were given. More hugs ensued. And then the two librarians slipped out the door.

"Well." Libby squared her slender shoulders and drew an innervating breath. "There's never a dull moment around here."

"The people of this community have come to rely on you," he said.

Unhappiness glimmered in Libby's green eyes as she regarded him. "That's not what I need to hear."

He had hurt her. Again. Without meaning to do so. He injected as much gentle levity into his tone as he dared. "What *do* you need to hear, then?"

She snorted indignantly. "Oh, something along the lines of you understand that although I have done everything I could to live up to the wishes of Percy and his parents in maintaining the Lowell family tradition and legacy in Laramie…you also know I'm leading a life I never intended to lead."

"I thought you liked running the dealership." She was certainly good at it.

She peered at him through narrowed lashes. "I like managing things, keeping things running and solving problems. I have no passion for farm and ranch equipment, per se."

He flashed her a cryptic smile. "You don't dream about combines and harvesters?"

Contrary as ever around him, she replied, "I have the occasional *nightmare* about a delivery not arriving in time for a rancher to harvest the crop that's going to feed his cattle all winter."

Holden cleared his throat, regarding her steadily. "You're serious."

She wandered back into the living room and plopped down on the sofa with her book. "Oh, yes."

He watched her slide her reading glasses back on her nose. "You never said anything."

She winced again. "That would have been ungrateful, wouldn't it?" Libby paused in the act of opening her novel. "Here I am, having inherited a beautiful home, a thriving business and the mantle of the esteemed Lowell name."

Holden sat opposite her and studied the elegant contours of her face.

"When all I really want, if I'm to be perfectly honest…" Libby raked her teeth across the velvety pink softness of her lower lip.

He gripped the arms of the chair and rocked forward slightly, guessing, "All you really want is your husband back."

A pained silence fell between them. When she spoke again, her defenses were up. "We both wish that were possible."

"I'm sorry, Libby."

"Please." She lifted a delicate palm. "Don't apologize. Not again…"

How could he not? Holden thought with a fresh flood of guilt. "If Percy and I hadn't gone on that white-water rafting trip in South America right after my marriage busted up…"

The light faded from her eyes. "He knew you were devastated when you lost the baby and Heidi, all at once."

The reminder of his loss had a wealth of undercurrents. "I never should have married her."

Libby sighed, perceptive as ever. "That's true, since

shotgun weddings have a very low success rate. But," she continued with laudable understanding, "you're a noble guy…and you were head over heels in love with her."

Holden folded his arms over his chest. "Even if it turns out Heidi didn't feel the same way." To his ex-wife, he had been her rebound guy from another relationship.

"You did what you thought was the right thing, in marrying her," Libby soothed.

"And failed, anyway."

She nodded, recalling compassionately, "And Percy wanted to cheer you up."

Wearily, Holden shoved his fingers through his hair. "I should have said no."

"Then Percy would have gone alone."

Holden looked at her in disbelief.

Leaning forward, Libby took off her glasses and confided, "You weren't the only one unhappy at the time, Holden. Percy was feeling hemmed in. He was tired of running the dealership in the wake of his parents' death, tired of living the 'expected, ordinary' life. He needed that little burst of pure freedom."

Holden grimaced in regret. "But he had responsibilities. We both knew the Rio Suarez could be dangerous." Many of the rapids were a grade four plus…!

Libby shrugged, clearly not as inclined to rewrite history as Holden was. "If your raft hadn't started to take on water and collapse the exact moment you hit the rapids," she said with a resignation that came straight from her soul. "If Percy hadn't jumped to save you…"

"And succeeded," Holden stated hoarsely.

"He never would have slammed into those boulders himself, or broken his leg and nearly drowned, until you and guides saved him. He wouldn't have needed to go to the hospital in San Gil, which was miles away, over rough terrain. His wounds wouldn't have become infected, and he wouldn't have started running a fever."

"And begged me to watch over you."

Abruptly, Libby looked as numb as she had at the funeral. "Had none of that happened, Percy would have lived." She stood and gazed deep into Holden's eyes. "But he didn't." Restlessly, she paced the length of the room. "And now you and I are here. Dealing with the aftermath of my late husband's reckless nature, each and every day."

Holden caught up with her. "You have to know," he croaked, gripping her hands, "if I could take it all back…" *Make your life better. Make you happy again…*

"I know, Holden. You would." Libby squeezed his palms, then let go. Sadness glimmered in her green eyes as she confessed, "And I would, too. But we can't. Instead, we have to deal with the fact that around here, I will always be Percy's 'tragic' widow. The keeper of the Lowell legacy, and the go-to person for all community problems needing solving. Around here, I'll never be just me. The Libby who grew up in Austin, and who wants a different kind of life."

He sighed heavily, watching her pained expression as she continued speaking her mind.

"Just as you will always be remembered as the guy who got quickly and unceremoniously dumped after Heidi lost your baby. The difference is, you've always lived here. You have tons of family in the area. And a ranch that you've built that will be your legacy from here on out." She met his eyes. "Divorced or no, this is the life you are *supposed* to be leading. Mine was here only as long as Percy was alive."

She had thought this through, Holden realized in shock. "You're serious about moving on, then."

"After more than two years?" Libby put her glasses back on her nose. "Yes. Very."

"So if this Jeff Johnston comes in with a good offer..."

"Or even a decent one," she affirmed.

"You'll take it."

Libby nodded, keeping the wall around her heart intact. "And I'll sell the house, move on...and never look back."

Chapter Two

"You're sure this is going to be okay?" Rosa asked Libby nervously on Friday morning.

Libby nodded and waved the library employee toward the dealership showroom. "You can set up a return desk over there in the corner. The books on hold—and the checkout and information counter—can go next to that."

Miss Mim came to join them. She'd brought with her a small army of library volunteers carrying armloads of supplies, boxes of books, even a computer. "Hopefully, we won't need to be here more than a couple of days."

Libby smiled at both librarians. "I'm sure we'll get this straightened out by then. In the meantime, library patrons will have a place to go for the essentials and information."

The dealership business was carrying on as usual. Two ranchers were in the offices, signing papers on new tractors and equipment. Another three were lined up to arrange service on their machines. And Lucia Gordon, the receptionist, was headed straight for Libby, a handsome thirtysomething man in a tweed sport coat and jeans by her side.

The tall stranger smiled as he reached her and held out his hand. "Libby Lowell, I presume?"

She grinned back. "The one and only."

He shook her hand. "Jeff Johnston."

Libby's jaw dropped in surprise. "I thought we weren't meeting until this evening."

"I wanted to let you know I had arrived and checked in at the Laramie Inn." Jeff looked around. "Plus I thought it would be good to see the place through the eyes of a regular customer." His brow furrowed as he noticed the temporary library being set up. "What's going on over there?"

Libby noted he didn't look pleased. Briefly, she explained the problem, as well as her solution, adding, "That's the way things work in a small town. We all go the extra mile to help each other out."

Jeff rubbed a hand across his jaw, considering that. "None of the customers seem to mind."

But, Libby noted, the next man coming into the dealership seemed wary. Not of what was going on in the corner, but of the man she was standing with.

Holden reached her and nodded at Jeff. "Johnston."

"McCabe."

Libby fought off a second wave of surprise. She squared her slender shoulders. "You two know each other?"

An inscrutable glint appeared in Holden's eyes as he informed her casually, "We met a little while ago at the Daybreak Café."

Which wasn't surprising, Libby guessed, since the restaurant owned by Holden's sister, Emily, was *the* place in town to have breakfast.

"I was chatting up the locals, asking around, to see how people felt about the dealership," Jeff explained.

Libby tensed, not sure how she felt about that. Shouldn't any questions have been directed at her first?

"Anyway, we're still on for dinner this evening, right?" Jeff asked.

She nodded.

"Great. I've got a lot of questions and things I'd like to discuss." He inclined his head and strolled off.

Holden gave Libby a steady look that sent heat spiraling through her. "Tell me you're taking someone with you. Like a lawyer."

Clearly, Holden didn't trust Jeff Johnston. For reasons that had more to do with his loyalty to her late husband— and to her—than to Johnston's overarching ambition, she suspected.

Libby folded her arms and moved closer to him. "I'm not paying a lawyer to sit through polite get-to-know-each-other chitchat."

Holden looked at her soberly. "Obviously, Johnston wants it to be more than that. He appears anxious to get you to sign on the dotted line, here and now."

She stepped back. "Then Mr. Johnston will be disappointed," she said firmly, uncomfortably aware that she'd had the same impression of the businessman. "But if it will make you feel better…you can tag along," she offered reluctantly.

Holden grinned as happily as if she had invited him into her bedroom. "Seriously?"

Doing her best to quell her conflicting emotions, Libby nodded. She did not want to depend on Holden, emotionally or otherwise. She had allowed herself to do that once, right after her husband's passing, and the result had been disastrous for both of them. To the point that guilt and discomfort from that time were still with both of them.

But she was smart enough to know that the easiest way to keep one man from becoming too aggressive with her was to put another equally driven and protective man into the mix. So for now, for tonight, she would allow her late husband's best friend to appease his conscience by employing his innate gallantry on her behalf, once more.

Having decided that, she sighed.

Glancing up at Holden, she couldn't help but note how good he looked in that green corduroy shirt and jeans. His short dark hair was thick and rumpled, and his face had the shadow of beard that came from going twenty-four hours without a razor. But it was the cobalt-blue of his eyes, the compassionate set of his sensual lips, that really drew her in.

"Thanks for inviting me," he said.

Libby gave him a glance that warned him not to get too carried away. "It makes more sense to have you at the table with us than to have you hovering somewhere in the background, trying to watch over me from a distance." Which, she knew, he was likely to do, given the depth of his concern about the potential pitfalls of the situation she was in.

And if she was completely honest, Libby admitted, she wouldn't mind having Holden at the first official meeting.

The handsome rancher was bound to be a lot less emotional about the proposed transaction than she, and would give her perspective on everything said.

In certain situations, two were better than one.

This, Libby figured, was one of those times.

"I DIDN'T REALIZE THE TWO of you were dating," Jeff Johnston said to Holden and Libby after they had ordered their meals.

Taking comfort in the laid-back ease of the Wagon

Wheel Restaurant, she sipped her iced tea. "Holden is here as a friend."

Jeff quirked a brow. "Do you always take friends to business meetings?"

Aware that her throat still felt parched, and that she was far too conscious of Holden and his sexy masculine presence, Libby took another drink. "No."

Jeff glanced at her curiously. "Then...?"

She searched for an explanation for herself, as well. Ignoring Holden's equally probing look, she told Jeff, "You wanted to know how the ranchers in the area feel about the dealership. Holden can tell you that."

The other man turned to him. "How is the level of service?"

"Excellent," Holden stated promptly. "First and foremost, prices are fair."

"Almost too much so," Jeff countered. "Since the profit the company is taking on sales is slightly below the industry standard."

"It's a competitive market," Libby interjected. "We aim to please."

"And they do," Holden said candidly. "From the time you walk in the door, Lowell Ranch Equipment employees are there to help you decide what heavy machinery you need, and how to obtain financing. And they are just as dedicated when it comes to providing any service or parts required. Because of that, they have a very loyal customer base."

"You're not just saying that because Libby is your 'friend'?" Jeff chided.

"Libby doesn't need me to exaggerate on her behalf," Holden said, beginning to sound a little irked at the remark. "Lowell Ranch Equipment has been in business for three generations, and has served a hundred-mile rural area for the last seventy years. The commitment of the sales and service staff has never wavered."

Jeff nodded, as if his research had garnered the same data. "I notice a lot of the employees are older, though. Fifty plus..."

For the thirtysomething Jeff, that was a problem, Libby noted unhappily. "Ten of our employees are in that age demographic—they have worked at the business their whole adult lives. Three others are in their twenties, but equally as committed to careers with us."

He frowned. "Meaning you would be opposed to me letting at least some members of your staff go, and bringing in my own people?"

She stiffened her spine, the tough businesswoman inside her coming to the fore. "I won't sell to you unless there is a guarantee you'll continue to employ every person currently working there for as long as they want to stay, at their current salary and benefits."

"You realize that could sour the deal," Jeff warned.

Libby turned her hands palm up. "Then it does."

He sat back in his chair as their dinners were put in front of them, and considered her position. "Well, that explains why everyone is so loyal."

Libby picked up her knife and fork. "We've had virtually no turnover, because it is such a good place to work. The fact the customers know who they are going to be dealing with is a comfort to them. Everyone feels like family."

Jeff cut into his steak. "In my experience, business and personal affairs don't mix."

She took a bite of her grilled redfish. "That may be true in Houston. It's not the case in Laramie." She paused long enough to meet Holden's encouraging glance, then asked Jeff, "Why do you want LRE so badly?" He had been calling her every few months since Percy died, asking if she wanted to sell.

He added butter to his baked potato. "I specialize in acquiring businesses with no internet presence and taking them online. LRE would be my biggest acquisition yet. I see great potential for growth. In fact, you could stay on if you want, Libby, because I'm not going to be there more than once a week—if that—and I'll need someone to manage it."

"Thank you for the offer, but—no. I'm selling because I want out."

"You're planning to leave the area, then?"

Out of the corner of her eye, Libby saw Holden tense. "Yes."

Jeff leaned toward her. "What about the house? Are you interested in including it in the sale? 'Cause I'm going to need someplace nice to stay when I'm in town."

Libby hesitated. How did she feel about that? "We could negotiate," she said cautiously. "If the price is right, of course."

"Can I see it tonight?" Jeff asked eagerly, while Holden tensed even more.

Ignoring his obvious disapproval, Libby shrugged. "I suppose a brief tour would be okay."

Victorious, Jeff smiled. "Then let's do it!"

They talked more as they ate. No one wanted dessert, so as soon as the check was paid, they went out to their vehicles. Libby took the lead in her Range Rover, with Jeff following in his Maserati and Holden trailing behind in his pickup truck.

Her self-appointed protector looked even grimmer when they arrived at the house.

The first thing that caught Jeff's eye was the Lowell photo gallery that lined much of the foyer and both walls of the grand front staircase. "Wow." He stopped at the framed pictures of three generations of Lowells, then he studied Percy and Libby's wedding photo.

"You were awfully young when you got married."

She had been. "Twenty-two. Right out of college."

"And you were married how long?"

Libby noticed Holden studying the photos, too, with the familiar mixture of grief, guilt and sadness. "Almost eight years."

Jeff turned back to her. "I can see why you want to sell," he told her empathetically. "Residing here must feel like living in a mausoleum."

Aptly put, Libby thought.

"The tour?" Holden said, looking irritated again.

Libby inhaled and braced herself for another slew of questions from the ambitious businessman. "Let's get started," she said. *So I can put this evening—and the onslaught of confusing emotions—behind me.*

HOLDEN KNEW LIBBY WAS ticked off at him. And maybe he was overstepping his bounds. But when Jeff Johnston asked to see the second floor…

"Not a good idea." Holden moved to block the way to the stairs.

Jeff turned to Libby with a goading smile. "I thought the two of you weren't involved."

"We're not," she said, a hint of color coming into her cheeks.

Maybe not in the traditional way, Holden thought. But

they were linked through Percy's memory. And he had made a promise not to let anyone take advantage of his best friend's widow. A promise he would continue to carry out until his dying day.

"Actually, we are," he stated flatly.

Libby's jaw dropped in shock. "I can't believe you just alluded to that," she said, glaring at Holden.

It didn't matter, he thought, because Jeff clearly believed him, not Libby. And Johnston's obvious respect for another man's territory would keep him from making an untoward pass at Libby, at least for now.

"I'm going to head out," Jeff said, his demeanor slightly less personal as he backed off. "But I'll be in touch."

"I look forward to it." Libby's tone was crisp and businesslike. Spine stiff, she walked him to the door.

As soon as he'd left, she whirled back to Holden and inhaled, the action lifting the soft curves of her breasts. A pulse worked in her throat as she kept her eyes meshed with his. "You had no right to tell Jeff Johnston he couldn't go up to the second floor."

Holden found himself tracking the fall of honey-colored hair swinging against her shoulders and caressing the feminine lines of her face. Wondering if it was as silky to the touch as he recalled, he asked, "You were really going to let Jeff Johnston see the bedrooms?"

"No, of course not." Libby propped her hands on her hips and sent him a chastising look. "Not without having a chance to tidy up and get the property ready to show!" She inched closer, inundating him with a drift of cinnamon perfume. "But that's not the point, Holden."

Desire sprang up within him, as surely as irritation had. Reminding himself she was off-limits for a whole host of reasons, he returned carefully, "Then what is the point?"

Their eyes locked, providing another wave of unbidden heat between them. "You intimated to him that you and I are having a fling."

"No." Holden savored her nearness, and the pleasure that came from being alone with her, in a way they hadn't been for months now.

He turned and wandered toward the cozy family room in the back of the house. "I said we are involved," he corrected, as he passed another row of photos, of Percy and Libby together, involved in all the outdoor activities Percy loved.

Reminded that Libby was once his best friend's wife, Holden shoved his hands in the pockets of his wool trousers and drawled, "I just didn't say *how* we are involved."

She stepped out of her heels and stood holding the sexy shoes, as if she wanted to lob them at his head. "Same difference," she snapped.

Holden let his glance drift down her spectacular pantyhose-clad legs to her toes. "Really?" His gaze returned slowly and deliberately to her face, pausing on her lips, before moving to her long-lashed green eyes. Ignoring the threat of the stilettos, he leaned closer still and dropped his tone to a husky whisper. "'Cause I don't remember anything sexual or romantic happening between us."

Libby sniffed and sent him a quelling look. "Only because you came to your senses and put a stop to it."

Wanting something wasn't the same as *taking* it. Particularly when they both had been lost and hurting, searching for any way to end the pain.

As it turned out, Holden recalled soberly, neither of them could have lived with that.

Curtailing his rising emotions, he shrugged. "You said it was for the best."

Libby kept her distance, eventually drifting over toward the fireplace, where she pivoted, her back to the mantel. Raking her teeth across her lower lip, she admitted quietly, "And that was true. I wasn't myself that night."

For a long time, Holden had let himself believe that.

Now, cognizant of the tension that charged the air between them, he studied the mixture of regret and longing in her eyes. Found himself theorizing before he could stop himself, "And maybe you were yourself, Libby. Maybe your instincts *were* right."

Another shadow crossed her eyes. "What are you saying?"

Holden looked at the gold broken-heart pendant shimmering against the delicate ivory of her skin. Lower still, he could see the hint of cleavage in the V neckline of her black cashmere sweater dress. "That if I hadn't been such a gentleman... If I had allowed us to follow through on our urges..."

Maybe she wouldn't have held him at arm's length all this time. Maybe they could have shrugged off that flare of desire and gone back to being friends. Kissed and found out there was no chemistry between them, after all. Or argued and cleared the tension that way.

Instead, they had been adult about it. Distant. Careful. Unerringly polite. And tense as could be.

Libby studied him with a brooding look. "I know you're trying to be gallant here, Holden. But we have to face facts. I was the one who wanted to kiss you that night. Not the other way around."

Noting the raw vulnerability in her expression, Holden felt his heart go out to her all over again.

He realized it was his turn to be honest. No matter how

much it complicated their lives. "You're wrong about that, Libby," he told her hoarsely.

His gaze lingered on her, as he paused to let his words sink in. "I would have given everything I had that night to see where that burst of physical attraction would lead."

She shook her head. "But we couldn't because I was a wreck. In some ways I still am a wreck."

Not sure what she meant, Holden stared at her.

Libby lifted her hands. "It's this house, Holden. The dealership. I can't be either place without feeling like Percy's wife." Her voice caught and her lower lip trembled. "That's the real reason I can't stay here in Laramie. If I do, I'll never be able to move on."

As Holden looked around, he saw what she meant.

The home was brimming with signs of Percy and his folks, and the generations who had lived here before that.

It was clearly a Lowell domain.

Holden recalled that Libby had suggested a few small changes after they had taken over the residence, when Percy was still alive. All had been gently but firmly refused. Libby, in her usual genial way, had stopped bringing up the subject. And although she could have redecorated since Percy died, she hadn't. Probably because it would have felt disloyal, an insult to his memory, or disrespectful to his wishes.

No wonder she felt trapped, Holden mused sympathetically. He edged closer. "You want to get married again?"

Determination stiffened her slender frame. "Of course. I want to fall in love. I want to have kids. I want to feel like everything good is still ahead of me."

Everything she would have had, Holden thought, on a fresh wave of guilt, had her husband still been alive.

"Then you're going to have to do a lot more than just sell

the dealership and the house," he told her sternly. "You're going to have to start dating again."

Libby eyed him mockingly. "Thank you, Dr. Phil."

"I'm serious."

"I know you are." Her hips swaying provocatively, she strode past him toward the kitchen.

Like every other room in the house, it had been decorated long before Libby arrived on the scene. And although the color scheme was okay—if you liked bleached oak cabinets and beige walls—the once top-of-the-line appliances were definitely showing their age. As were some of the wall hangings and wooden blinds.

"The only problem is, no one will ask me out."

She hit the switch, flooding the room with light, then headed for the fridge.

Holden followed her lazily. Glad she had decided to do something to distract them from the new tension between them, he watched her rummage through the contents until she emerged with a chocolate-and-peppermint Yule log from the local bakery.

His mouth watering for more than the sweet, he settled against the counter.

"That's because you're still putting out the I'm-a-widow-and-therefore-off-limits-to-anyone-with-any-sensitivity vibe."

Libby stood on tiptoe to reach the dessert plates. "I am not."

He came forward to help her, steadying her with a hand to her waist. "Yeah...you are." He finished getting the dishes down for her. "But we can fix that."

Her lips pursed stubbornly. "How?" she asked, cutting two slices and handing him one, complete with a fork.

Holden settled opposite her at the table. Their knees

touched momentarily. Regretting the contact—and the sizzle of warmth it engendered—he pulled back and continued to focus on solving her problem. "By finding you a rebound guy."

Libby frowned. "I get that you're trying to help me, but why would you want any other guy to sign up for that—after what you went through with your ex?" She scowled protectively, like the close friend she had once been before their ill-fated kiss-that-never-quite-happened. "Heidi broke your heart! To the point that you've never dated seriously since."

"I haven't dated seriously because I haven't found the right woman," Holden corrected bluntly. "But I should put myself out there if I want to move on, too. And I do."

Libby went very still. "What are you suggesting?"

Holden's spirits rose as the idea took on momentum. "That we both shake off the rust. Get back in the game."

Libby licked the frosting off the back of her fork. "By that you mean…?"

"Go out to dinner. Attend holiday parties. Really celebrate the season. Who knows? If you and I get back in the habit of dating again, it might give us both a whole new outlook on life."

Libby's soft lips took on an enticing curve. "Meaning what?" she murmured cynically. "I might be so content I won't want to sell the dealership and move out of town?"

He grinned at her sarcasm and lifted a palm. "I'm just saying…"

Silence fell as the notion stuck. They studied each other.

Libby took the last bite of her dark chocolate cake, savoring the sweet decadence. "So, cowboy with all the answers, how do you propose I find my rebound man?"

Chapter Three

"You're looking at him."

Libby stared at Holden, sure she hadn't heard right. "Why in the world would you do that, after the way you were hurt the last time?"

"Unwittingly being someone else's rebound person is what makes me right for the task. I know you still love Percy and always will. It's not going to be easy for you to move on."

Guilt threatened to overwhelm Libby. She and Percy *hadn't* been in love at the end. But no one knew that…. "Don't put me up for sainthood," she said quietly. She had enough of that from the community every single day. "Because I'm not the perfect woman and I was never the perfect wife."

"Percy sure thought otherwise."

More guilt flooded her heart.

"He'd never met a woman who was more accommodating."

Libby pushed back her chair and carried her plate to the dishwasher. "Which is one reason I'm so unhappy," she remarked lightly. "I've spent too much of my life trying to please everyone else."

Holden put his dish and fork in the machine, too. Then

he leaned against the counter, watching her. "Your aunt Ida?"

Libby could feel him sizing her up, trying to figure out how to convince her to stay where he could keep an eye on her, and hence, continue to fulfill his deathbed promise to her late husband.

Wishing she weren't so aware of Holden's presence, Libby retreated into scrupulous politeness. "I was only seven when my parents died. Even though my aunt was in her fifties at the time, she took on the responsibility of raising me." She sighed. "I loved her dearly and will always be grateful to her for taking me in. But…because I was her only remaining family and she mine…she was paranoid about potential dangers and kept me on a very tight leash."

"I remember you had to live at home with her while you were attending UT."

Promising herself she was not going to fall prey to the attraction between them, Libby nodded. "Part of it was that she needed someone to take care of her by then, but the other part was that she didn't want me doing anything the least bit reckless."

"Which is where Percy came in," Holden guessed.

Libby made a face. In retrospect she could hardly believe her recklessness. "After Aunt Ida passed, that was all I wanted to do. Percy took me skydiving and hiking and taught me how to water-ski." More than anything, the diversion had helped her survive her mourning.

Holden moved closer, holding her gaze in an increasingly intimate way. "You don't do any of that stuff anymore."

Hanging on to her composure by a thread, she rubbed a nick on the counter with her fingertip. "I guess I had more of my aunt in me than I realized because I never really liked it."

Any more than I like selling tractors and ranch equipment now.

"But…at the same time—" Libby lifted her chin, drew a deep breath "—I had something to prove. Once that was accomplished, my total freedom to finally do as I pleased verified that I actually wanted a more sedate lifestyle." She flashed him a rueful smile, aware that what had comforted her had eventually ended up nearly doing him in. "Which was where you entered the picture…."

"I went back to doing those things with Percy when you stopped."

"And—contrary to what you might have thought—I really was appreciative."

"That I took your place?"

"I knew Percy wasn't going to stop indulging in physically challenging activities. He was too much of a daredevil for that. I was glad he had someone trustworthy and levelheaded to go with him."

Holden's expression radiated guilt, and silence fell between them.

Compassion for his plight forced her to go on. "So you see, Holden," Libby continued gently, "you have already done more than enough for both Percy and for me. You really don't have to squire me around, the way you did tonight."

"Suppose I want to," Holden said. "What then?"

She blinked. "Why would you want to do that?" she demanded.

Merriment turned up the corners of his lips. "Because it occurs to me now that I need a rebound woman as much as you need a rebound man."

HER HEARTBEAT KICKING UP a notch, Libby studied him. "You're serious."

Holden lounged against the counter opposite her, his arms folded against his chest. He stared at her with a steely resolve that matched her own. "Think about it. I'll always view you as Percy's wife."

Trying not to think what his steady appraisal and deep voice did to her, Libby appraised him right back. "And I'll always regard you as his best friend."

Cynicism twisted a corner of his mouth. "So there's no chance either of us will take a dating arrangement to heart."

Libby began to see where he was going with this. His proposal could be the solution to both their problems, as well as a bridge to the future. "It'll just be part of the process we both need to go through to get back out there."

"Right," he said casually. "Kind of like riding a bike..."

Stubbornly, she kept her eyes locked with his, even as her heart raced like a wild thing in her chest. "We're going to need ground rules," she warned.

He accepted her condition with a matter-of-fact nod. "The more specific, the better."

"How long should we do this?"

He shrugged, considering. "Through New Year's?"

Libby drummed her fingers on the countertop. "That would get us all the way through the holidays."

His big body began to relax. "It's always good not to be alone this time of year."

She nodded and took a deep breath. "Invites too much pity. Which—" she leaned in close "—is something I think we can agree neither of us needs."

A companionable silence fell between them. Searching

for other pitfalls, Libby said, "What about our friends and your family?"

Holden grimaced, suddenly looking like a knight charged with protecting his queen. "I don't see any need to make a big announcement. They'll figure it out. Eventually."

She appreciated his desire to shield her from hurt. And while she didn't need his chivalry, in this one instance she supposed it wouldn't hurt to accept it. "That would lessen the pressure."

"And perhaps the scrutiny, as well."

He was right in that respect. There was nothing worse than having everyone tracking the progress of a new romance, and then broadcasting the "latest developments" to everyone they knew.

"What about sex?" Libby pressed, perfectly willing to keep their process of renewal private. "Because if you're expecting to go to bed with me as part of our bargain…"

Holden winced, as if he found the whole idea painful and awkward. "I don't think we need to make it a condition of the relationship," he interjected swiftly.

Libby breathed a sigh of relief.

"On the other hand…" he continued with a wicked smile. He was ready for whatever came.

Was she?

Hit with a sudden case of nerves, Libby cleared her throat. "I'm not sure I…" She stopped, unable to go on. There were shortcomings she did not wish to discuss. Her ability to hold a man's attention in the bedroom topped the list.

Holden frowned, all protective male again. "Then don't worry about it," he said, his gaze sincere. "We're only going to be together for six weeks. Then we'll be moving on. Frankly, it might be better for our friendship if we didn't consummate the dating thing."

Libby relaxed again. "Thank you."

Not that she was surprised. Holden McCabe was always a true gentleman.

"Is it true?" Several LRE employees confronted Libby the next morning the minute she walked in the front door. "Are you really planning to sell Lowell Ranch Equipment?"

Lucia Gordon, the dealership receptionist, wrung her hands. "We figured you were just talking to Jeff Johnston to price him out of the market and get him to stop calling you."

"Today, I've already had requests from him to fax all the financials over to him at the Laramie Inn, ASAP," Vince Hunt reported.

Libby directed the group into her private office, where everyone stood shoulder to shoulder. She put down her purse and coffee mug. "He should not have asked you that. He should have come through me for any further information he needed."

"Percy left the dealership to you because you're the last of the Lowells and he expected you to take care of it," Manny Pierce reminded her. "Not end three generations of Lowell family tradition and cash in." The senior mechanic frowned. "We're really disappointed in you, Libby."

"As well as worried about our jobs," Swifty Mortimer added.

Libby worked her coat off and slung it over the back of her desk chair. "No one is going to lose their employment over this. That I can promise you."

Skeptical glances abounded. Clearly disgruntled, everyone filtered out.

The rest of the workday went just as badly.

Near 4:00 p.m., Libby walked over to the warehouse to do the end of November inventory.

She had just climbed into the cab of a deluxe combine harvester to compare the serial number and price with the information they had in their computer system when Holden McCabe walked into the building.

How was it, she wondered, that he knew intuitively just when to show up to save the day or lighten her mood? Despite her decision not to rely on him emotionally in any way, her heart gave a little leap.

Oblivious to the hopelessly dependent nature of her thoughts, Holden lifted one brawny arm in acknowledgment. He strode confidently toward her.

Her heart took another little leap of anticipation as he neared.

Appearing concerned, he climbed into the enclosed cab beside her and shut the door.

His shoulder and hip brushed hers as he settled onto the bench seat. "What's going on?" he asked her as he shot her another concerned look.

Trying not to notice how much space his tall, muscular frame took up, Libby swallowed. She hadn't wanted to cry on his shoulder this much since the night he had brought her home from the emergency room.

She drew another breath as her pulse picked up a notch and a guilty flush heated her face. "Pretty much what you'd expect, under the circumstances. All the employees are mad at me. They think I'll be betraying the Lowells if I sell."

He studied her empathetically. "Sometimes you have to forget pleasing everyone else and make yourself happy." He shrugged and briefly squeezed her forearm. "I'm thinking this is one of those times."

Libby released a tremulous breath and raked a hand through her hair. "You really do understand." And she needed that. Even though she was convinced she was doing the right thing, this situation left her feeling more vulnerable than she had expected.

With a cajoling smile, and another pat on her arm, Holden predicted, "And everyone else will understand, too, given a little time. In the meantime—" he released her and sat back "—I've got some more bad news—if you think you can handle it."

Aware how her arm was tingling from that brief, comforting touch, Libby turned her attention to the rotary thresher attached to the front of the machine. She took a second to brace herself for the second onslaught of the day. "Go ahead," she instructed wearily.

He rested a powerful forearm on the hydraulic steering wheel. "The library has been closed indefinitely. Apparently, what Rowdy found beneath the subflooring was asbestos that had been used for electrical insulation and soundproofing."

Libby winced. "That sounds dangerous."

He nodded. "It can be a real health hazard if it starts to deteriorate, and this stuff looked pretty old." Cheering slightly, he added, "The good news is all the AC filters and surfaces in the library building tested clean of any microscopic fibers that could be inhaled, so no one's been in danger thus far. But it's going to have to come out."

She sighed wearily as she waited for him to continue.

He met her level gaze. "And it's going to be a very expensive proposition. The initial estimate from the hazardous-material experts is a quarter of a million, and the county doesn't have it in the budget."

Libby's heart sank as she contemplated the loss. "So what are they going to do?"

"Try and find the money somewhere, but the earliest that will happen is January."

She clapped a hand over her heart. "And in the meantime?"

"The county is arranging for Laramie residents to have privileges in neighboring county library systems."

"But those are thirty-five miles away, minimum!" Libby declared in dismay.

Holden exhaled, looking disappointed, as well. "It's the best the county can do."

She turned toward him urgently, her knee bumping his thigh in the process. "There has to be a better solution!" she protested hotly.

The corners of his lips curved upward. "Miss Mim and Miss Rosa are collecting suggestions as we speak." His glance sifted slowly over Libby's face, lingering on the flush in the cheeks and her lush bare lips, before returning to her eyes. "In the meantime, I was thinking. It is Saturday...so how about tonight for our first official date?"

HOLDEN WAS SURPRISED but pleased that Libby assented right away. "The distraction might be just what I need...."

He'd half feared she would get cold feet about the whole arrangement and try to beg off, but she hadn't, so they agreed to meet at her house at seven-thirty.

Leaving her to finish the inventory, Holden went home to the Bar M ranch to take care of his horses, shower and change. Figuring there would be less pressure on them if they had dinner and saw a movie, he printed out the listings for the theater in town and the multiplex in San Angelo, then headed back to Libby's place.

He stared at the vehicles lining her driveway and clogging the parking lot of the now-closed dealership across the road.

Her home, he soon found out, was just as congested.

Twenty-five or so women were crowded into the spacious living room. Miss Mim and Miss Rosa were holding court.

The topic? The library, of course.

"The problem is," Rosa was saying as Holden took off his coat and joined the group, "there's no available building in Laramie where three floors of books could be housed temporarily."

"I have an idea," Libby said. "It's a little unusual, but…"

All eyes turned to her.

"What if we divided the books up into sections, much the way they are now, and looked for host homes in town to function as mini-libraries? We could put the information online and still have a help desk in the LRE showroom. Hours could be limited. Say two hours, three times a week, max, for each farmed-out section of the library. That way, the books would still be available to local residents, and they wouldn't have to travel to a neighboring county."

"What an amazing idea!" Miss Mim said.

Holden thought so, too.

The room erupted in applause.

More excited talk ensued.

Holden's sister, Emily, appeared at his side. "Libby is quite the heroine, isn't she?"

"Yes," he murmured, "she is."

Not that this was a surprise. It didn't matter what the problem was. Whether it be a personal or civic matter,

Libby was always first in line to help. The first to start or lead a crusade. Everyone in Laramie knew that, which was why the library volunteers and personnel had convened here tonight. Because they had known that when presented with a particularly thorny problem, Libby Lowell would know just what to do.

Holden couldn't help but admire Libby as she confidently held court. She wasn't just gorgeous as all get-out. She was smart and kind, and could think outside the box.

In fact, he had never met a more fascinating woman in his life. And if she hadn't started out as his best friend's girl, he might have pursued her himself.

His sister broke through his reverie. "And if I didn't know better—" Emily smiled and playfully punched Holden's arm "—I'd think *you* had a thing for her."

"WHAT WERE YOU AND EMILY talking about?" Libby asked, after everyone had left.

She thinks I am falling for you. Which is ridiculous, since at the end of the day I'll still see you as the woman who was once married to my best friend.

Pretty sure Libby was not ready to hear any of that, Holden shrugged indolently and cut to the chase. "Like everyone else I know, my sister wants me to get out there and start dating again."

Libby kept her eyes on his a disconcertingly long time, then lifted her chin and regarded him suspiciously. "Did you tell her about us?"

Holden tried not to notice how much trouble she had gone to for their "first date." She had put on a ruffled Western blouse, formfitting brown cords and lace-up tan boots. Her hair had been swept up into a loose, sexy knot on the back of her head, her lips softly glossed. She smelled of her trademark cinnamon-and-spice perfume. He forced himself to sound as casual as they'd agreed they would be.

"I figured we would actually go out first." *See how it went.* "Speaking of which…"

"I know." The enticing curves of her breasts pushed against the fabric of her blouse as she inhaled. "I'm sorry." Her tiny reindeer earrings jangled as she tilted her head slightly to one side. "I didn't mean for that to happen, but when Miss Mim and Rosa called, wanting to brainstorm and bring along a few others, I couldn't say no."

Holden's glance fell to the delicate hollow of Libby's throat before returning to her eyes. "I understand."

She raked her teeth over her luscious lower lip. "I didn't expect it to go on so long."

Aware he was beginning to get aroused—also not part of their bargain—he glanced at his watch. "It's only nine-thirty. We could still do something." Anything to kill the desire building within him.

"Like what?" Libby moved around the room, picking up a few stray glasses and plates. "The late movies have already started."

She hurried past him, her long, sexy strides adding fuel to the fire already burning deep inside him.

"And most of the restaurants are already closing down. Not that I'm hungry—" Libby chattered on, setting the items in the sink "—since everyone who came over brought some sort of food."

Holden caught up with her and put the things he had gathered down, too.

Aware she looked increasingly tense and worried—as if afraid to be alone with him—he put his hands on her shoulders. "Relax."

She tensed even more at his touch. "Sorry." Swallowing, she forced a nervous smile, stepped back.

This would not do.

Holden shook his head in mute rebuke. Using humor to ease the sudden stress, he winked. "You're as skittish as a cat who just had her tail caught beneath a rocking chair."

The comparison worked to quell her nerves. "Funny." Libby returned his droll look with one of her own.

"Seriously." Holden stepped back and suggested smoothly, "We could go out and get a beer. Listen to music at the dance hall."

Libby lifted an elegant brow. "And no doubt run into your mom—because she owns the place?"

He rubbed his hand across the back of his neck. "You're right," he admitted. "That would be a little claustrophobic for a first date. Even a very casual one."

Libby sighed and held up a hand in surrender. "Maybe we should just call it a night," she said apologetically. "Try again—I don't know—sometime next week."

Holden knew a woman about to back out on him when he saw one. He caught up with her in the hall and kept pace. "What's wrong with tomorrow?"

Libby frowned at the sight of a dirty glass she had missed. She picked it up and held it in front of her like a shield. "I'm going to be at the library to help remove the uncontaminated books that are coming to my home. After that, I'll be busy setting up temporary stacks in my living room."

"I can help with that," Holden volunteered.

She shook her head. "You don't have to."

He studied her, knowing they could not leave it like this and expect things to get any better between them. "I want to," he insisted quietly.

Libby seemed completely at a loss as to what to say or do next. Which in turn made Holden take a step closer, and ask, "Are you trying to get rid of me?" He scanned her head to toe, his eyes narrowed suspiciously. "Because you suddenly seem *very* nervous." And he wanted to know why…so it wouldn't happen again.

"I'm just wired," she said evasively, setting the lone glass on the foyer console rather than carry it all the way back to the kitchen. She jammed her hands on her hips. "It's been a long day. A lot has happened."

"Mmm-hmm." Holden studied her some more. "Sure it's not something else?" he prodded.

She widened her pretty eyes, all innocence. "Like what?" she asked with Texas belle sweetness.

And if there was one thing Libby was not, it was a coquette.

Holden stepped even closer. "Like the kiss…that *almost* happened. That is still on both our minds every time we are alone."

Color swept into Libby's cheeks. "So what if it is?" she taunted defiantly. "I'm sure we'll get rid of the notion sooner rather than later."

Holden grinned, the man in him rising to the womanly challenge in her. "I prefer sooner," he murmured.

Libby scoffed and tossed her head. "Well, so would I! But…there's no way to do that."

"Sure there is," Holden told her confidently. "I'll show you."

Chapter Four

Holden threaded his fingers through her hair, then bent and kissed first her temple and then her cheek.

"Trust me," he whispered, as his mouth drifted slowly, inevitably toward hers. "This is the only solution…if we're ever to have any peace…."

Much as she was loath to admit it, Libby knew he was right. Giving in to the curiosity that had been plaguing her for years now, she went up on tiptoe. Holden groaned, pulling her flush against him. Her heart racing, Libby parted her lips to the investigating pressure of his. He responded by kissing her even more deeply. Her entire body going soft with pleasure at the unhurried coaxing of his lips and the seductive stroking of his tongue, she wrapped her arms around his neck and tilted her hips to his.

For the first time in her life, she began to see what she'd been missing. This was the kind of kiss she had always dreamed about and never received. Evocative. Inundating. Tender. The kind that made her feel all woman to his man. The kind that made her feel that being close to someone again might not be such a crazy idea, after all….

HOLDEN HADN'T COME HERE tonight intending to kiss Libby. In fact, his plan had been to delay the physical indefinitely.

But that had been before he'd seen the veil come over her eyes yet again, in a way that made him wonder why intimacy of any kind with him was such a threat to her.

And suddenly he knew.

He broke off the kiss, dropped his arms to his sides and stepped back. "All this time I thought the reason you were so ill at ease with me was because we almost kissed." He paused, looking deep into her eyes. "But that isn't it at all. Is it?"

OF ALL THE THINGS she did not want to discuss, her foolish behavior had to be at the top of the list. "I was an idiot that night, long before I hurled myself at you." One giant mess of hormones and pent-up emotion.

He gave her an understanding glance. "You thought you were pregnant."

Misery engulfed her. "And I wasn't."

Holden caught her hand when she would have turned away. "But you didn't know that when you called me and asked me to drive you to the hospital." He squeezed her palm compassionately. "You thought you were losing your baby."

Libby leaned into his touch despite herself. "Had I been with child, that baby would have been three months along. Instead, all that was happening inside me was a lot of cramping and the beginning of the worst menstrual period ever! I've never felt so ridiculous or been so humiliated in my entire life."

Holden studied her. "And Paige and I witnessed it."

Libby struggled to get a grip. "The difference being that Paige is a physician and a woman." Her best friend had been able to view the situation with the clinical detachment that Libby had needed. Holden had reacted much more emotionally. Which had made her feel even worse about dragging him into the situation, and dumping all her problems on him.

"I never thought less of you." He wrapped his arms around her shoulders and pulled her close. "My heart went out to you that night," he murmured against the top of her head. "You'd just lost Percy a couple of months before, and when you thought you were having his baby, you had such joy." His warm breath touched her ear.

In an effort to shield her eyes from his probing gaze, she let her head rest against his chest. "And guilt, and a million other things," she whispered as a flood of tears pressed hotly behind her eyes.

He brought her closer yet, one hand moving down her back in long, soothing strokes. "Why guilt?"

Maybe it was time she began to unburden herself. And who better to tell than Holden, who had his own regrets?

Fighting the overwhelming sadness she felt whenever she thought of all that preceded and followed Percy's tragic death, she looked him in the eye and took another halting breath. Finally, she asked what she had never dared voice before. "You don't know the real reason Percy insisted on taking that trip to South America, do you?"

"He said it was to cheer me up after my divorce was final," Holden replied in a low, gravelly voice.

Libby dabbed at the moisture beneath her eyes. "Well, that was part of it," she said finally, drawing back.

He brought her back into the curve of his strong arms. His touch was more brotherly than anything else, despite their earlier flirtation with passion. "And the other…?" he murmured.

Libby struggled to get her emotions under control.

"Percy and I had been arguing about starting a family. I really wanted a baby."

Holden nodded, his grip tightening protectively.

"But Percy didn't." The tears she had been doing everything to block flowed anyway.

Holden frowned.

Libby pressed on the bridge of her nose to keep more tears from falling. "He already felt tied down." She gulped and forced herself to go on, get it all out. "He felt he had gotten a raw deal. Inheriting the responsibility for the family business years before he was ready to assume it. Having the woman he married turn out not to be so adventurous and wild at heart, after all. The last thing Percy wanted was the responsibility of a child. Not then, he said, maybe not ever." She shook her head, remembering that last awful fight. "I was devastated."

Holden exhaled. "And angry, I'm guessing."

She forced a watery smile, then she dabbed at her eyes again. "Very. The presumption that we would have children, if for no other reason than to carry on the Lowell name and bloodlines, had always been there."

She looked up at Holden, wanting him to understand. "Suddenly…with the death of his parents—and the absence of that familial pressure to produce grandkids—there was no reason in Percy's mind to go forward with a family at all. So he scheduled the trip with you to Colombia, and that was that. There was not going to be any more discussion about it when he came back.

"I was so angry and disappointed I didn't even kiss him goodbye before he left."

And then he had died….

Leaving her with even more to grapple with.

Holden shook his head. Swore softly. "Libby. I had no idea—"

She held up a hand. "I know—no one did." Feeling calmer now, she pulled away. "Anyway, that's why I had such a crazy mix of emotions when I suspected I might be pregnant after Percy died. I was happy about the baby, but knew he wouldn't have been. It felt like a miracle and a lifelong burden of guilt, all in one."

"Stress can do funny things to a person's body."

Libby nodded, appreciating Holden's attentiveness, even as she warned herself not to get too used to it.

Still, she needed to talk to him tonight. Needed the brand of comfort only he could give. "The doctors said my devastation over Percy's death and the acrimonious way we parted, combined with my longing for a child, made my hormones a mess. I was barely eating or sleeping. I was dizzy and nauseated, more often than not. And I went three months without a period before I realized it."

Holden reached over and tucked a strand of her hair behind her ear. "It's only natural you concluded what you did."

Silence fell between them as she looked deep into his eyes, noticing yet again what a ruggedly handsome man he was. It was more than just the symmetry of his features or the strong line of his jaw. It was his kindness and compassion. His easygoing attitude and humor. The way he could always make a person feel better with an offhand comment or smile.

"You really think that?"

"Yes. I do." He hugged her briefly.

She drew back again, feeling as if a weight had been lifted off her heart. "I'm glad we talked about this."

"So am I." He looked as if he, too, had felt a wall come tumbling down.

"But now we really have to call it a night." *Before I start making this into something more romantic and meaningful than it really is.*

His expression radiated a distinct male satisfaction as he prodded, "So, our first official rebound date…?"

"…will have to wait until we help Miss Rosa and Miss Mim temporarily relocate the Laramie Public Library," Libby finished firmly.

He squinted as if doing some mental calculations, then said, "Just so I know you're not backing out on our agreement."

"I'm not," she promised.

She just needed to make sure that when it did happen, she was composed enough to acknowledge the date for what it was.

Otherwise, it could mean trouble for both of them.

THE IMPROMPTU MEETING at Libby's home the evening before had involved mostly women. The gathering Sunday afternoon at the library was mostly of men. And for good reason, Libby thought, as she searched the sea of helpers for the person she most wanted to say hello to, since the task involved moving literally thousands of books to their temporary new homes.

"Looking for someone?" Paige teased, coming up to stand beside her.

Libby continued scanning the crowd. "Holden."

Her friend handed her a roll of tape, a marker and two collapsed cardboard boxes. "Not here yet. He should be soon, though." She guided Libby to the toddler section, where work was already under way. "What's going on with the two of you, anyway?"

Libby ducked her head and focused on putting the box together. "What do you mean?"

Paige pulled up a kid's chair and sank into it. "Why was he at your house last night, looking like he was ready to go out? And why were you so dressed up?"

Libby flushed. Leave it to her best friend...

"And speak of the devil," Paige murmured with a cheeky grin.

Libby turned to see Holden coming to join them. He had on an old UT sweatshirt and a pair of threadbare jeans, and he hadn't shaved. His dark hair had that rumpled, just-out-of-bed, can't-be-bothered-with-a-comb look, and he was carrying a tool belt in one hand, a pair of leather work gloves in the other. Her pulse raced at the sight of him. "Hi," she said, unable to help recalling the kiss they had shared.

He looked as if he was doing the same. Even though she had panicked and kicked him out early.

"Hi," he said, in a softer, sexier tone than usual.

Paige scoffed. "You can't tell me something *isn't* going on!"

Holden announced, deadpan, "We're going to date. We just haven't decided when."

"What?" She turned back to Libby. "Is he pulling my leg?"

Holden looked at Libby, daring her to deny it.

It was now or never, she thought. Time to jump in all the way.

Or let this chance to start moving on pass her by. She inhaled deeply, stepped closer to Holden and dived in. "We're talking about being each other's rebound date."

"That's the craziest thing I've ever heard!" Paige declared as her husband joined them.

"Crazy like a fox, maybe," Kurt declared in amusement.

Holden put on his tool belt. "All we're looking for is a short-term thing to get us over the hump."

Genuinely worried, Paige said, "Hearts get broken this way."

"Ours won't," Libby retorted, as Holden wrapped a companionable arm around her shoulders and gave her a reassuring squeeze.

NEVERTHELESS, an interesting question had been raised. And it stuck with Libby the rest of the afternoon.

"Do you think Paige was right?" she asked Holden much later, when they were working at her home.

Volunteers had moved the living-room furniture to the garage for safekeeping. The large space was now filled with the partially disassembled child-size tables and chairs, and the waist-high bookshelves that comprised the newborn to age three section of the library.

Holden opened a box labeled A-C and set it next to the appropriate shelf for her, then returned to his task of putting legs back on tables. "Paige wants us both to be happy. She's just not sure this is the way." He paused to drive in a screw with a battery-powered tool. Finished, he set the table right side up and turned to Libby with a smile. "I, on the other hand, think we've come up with a great plan to get ourselves back in the saddle."

His confidence was catching.

"You're right," she said, bolstering her courage. She knew Holden would never hurt her. She was foolish to worry.

AN HOUR LATER, the work was done and Libby and Holden stood back, admiring the newly assembled toddler section. It was just as it had been, Holden noted with satisfaction, right down to the wooden train table and the colorful charts and posters on display.

Looking flushed and disheveled, Libby turned to him. Her high ponytail bounced from side to side and she had dirt smudged across her casual cotton sweater and jeans. She had never looked prettier. "Did you eat anything at the library?

Holden shook his head. "I was too busy."

Admiring you...

"Then you must be starving. Because I am!"

Holden saw the opening and took it. He removed his tool belt and set it aside. "Want to go out?"

Libby looked down at herself and then him. He was just as grubby as she was. "Would you mind eating here?"

Was she kidding? She was a fantastic cook.

"Not at all." In fact, he was happy to see her feeling comfortable enough with him to invite him to stay. It reminded him of all the dinners he'd had there with her and Percy, before the accident. Some with Heidi, some without. It hadn't mattered. He'd always had a good time in Libby's kitchen. Maybe because she was like the women in his family, able to put people at ease....

She led the way back to the kitchen, where she turned on the oven and put a pan on the stove. Then waggled her eyebrows at him facetiously. "Have your culinary skills improved any?"

Was it Holden's imagination or was it already getting hot in here? He lounged against the counter, trying to stay out of her path. "I can boil water," he joked.

"Want to try and help me, anyway?"

This was something, Holden knew, that Percy had never been willing to do. "Sure," he said. If this was a test regarding his dating ability—as it suddenly seemed to be—he was determined to pass it.

"Okay, then." Libby got an armful of ingredients out of the fridge, another from the pantry. She paused to pull her V-neck sweater over her head and set it aside, then pushed the sleeves of her white long-sleeved T-shirt to her elbows. "I make soup every Sunday evening."

Holden tried not to notice how the cotton fabric clung to the curves of her breasts. "When did this start?"

"After Percy died. I couldn't seem to manage anything that required even a moderate amount of concentration. But soup was foolproof."

Holden chuckled. "Then it sounds like the perfect dish for me."

"Not to worry. I know it doesn't sound very filling, but I'll whip up some quesadillas for you, too. In the meantime—" she got out a bag of chips and a jar of salsa and arranged them on a serving dish "—you can munch on these, since our main course is going to take about an hour to prepare."

"Thanks."

"No problem." Looking increasingly at ease, she handed him a cutting board and knife. Then a green pepper, a red pepper, several ripe tomatoes and an onion. "Think you can chop these up into little pieces?"

It was his turn to smile. "Oh ye of little faith…"

Libby mugged comically as she started mixing chili powder, cumin and garlic powder, and the aroma of Southwestern spices filled the kitchen.

Enjoying the camaraderie that had sprung up between them, Holden cut the seeds and stem out of the peppers.

He was more awkward than she was, but could still get the job done. "I'm guessing we're making tortilla soup?" he asked eventually.

Purposefully, Libby lined up boneless chicken breasts on a rimmed baking sheet, drizzled on olive oil, sprinkled on spice and put that into the oven to bake. "You guessed right."

"Now what?" he said when he'd finished dicing.

She poured a little more olive oil in the bottom of the stockpot. The heat of the stove had her sculpted cheeks glowing pink. "Pour the veggies in here and then stir them around."

He tried not to think how much he had enjoying kissing her, or how sweet and feminine her body had felt pressed against his. Even now, he fought the urge to hold her in his arms again.

"You mean sauté them?"

Merriment danced in her green eyes. "You really aren't as unschooled as you look."

Holden laughed and started stirring as directed.

Shaking her head in amusement, Emily opened containers of chicken broth, tomatoes with jalapeño peppers and black beans. All were added to the sizzling veggies. The quarters were close, and Holden's shoulder nudged hers as they worked. "It's starting to look like soup." He could smell the chicken roasting, too.

"As soon as we put the meat in…" Libby paused.

His brow furrowed, Holden fixed his attention on the window above the kitchen sink.

She came closer, in a drift of soap and shampoo, and studied his face. "What are you looking at?"

Clearly, she didn't think there was much to notice in

the backyard. Especially at dusk on a cold winter's day. Holden frowned. "Was there snow in the forecast?"

Libby's shoulders brushed his. "There was a ten-percent chance of rain, but—"

He pointed toward the glass. "Does that look like rain to you?"

She stood on tiptoe to get a better view. "I don't know… it's so gloomy. How can you tell?"

"One way to find out." He headed for the back door.

As he had hoped, Libby was right behind him.

Laramie was far enough north that it snowed at least once a year, usually only a couple inches at a time. And it melted the next day. So this wouldn't be unprecedented.

Holden stepped off the porch and into the yard. He held his palms out, as did she. Sure enough, he realized with a smile, it was snow! Tiny white flakes that swirled in the wind and dotted their faces and hands.

Libby laughed in delight, her voice soft and musical, and maybe the best thing he'd heard in a long time. "Wow," she exclaimed, even as she shivered in the cold winter air. "It never snows this early in December."

Holden wished he had a jacket to put over her. The best he could do was wrap his arm around her shoulder and draw her in close. "It's doing it now," he said, laughing in turn.

She leaned against him as they stared up in wonder, watching it snow.

"It's not going to stick, but…" Libby turned toward him, as captivated by the magic of the moment as he was. "I still can't believe it," she murmured, looking deep into his eyes.

Holden brushed snowflakes from her hair. "Believe it,"

he said. And then he did what he'd wanted to do all day. He pulled her against him and kissed her again.

Her lips softened, yet were not quite pliant. She wreathed her arms about his neck and pressed close, as if savoring his warmth and his strength, but not sure if she should let it go any further, or open up the floodgates.

Even so, it was all the encouragement he needed. He cupped her face in his hands and deepened the kiss, wondering all the while what it would take to make her feel as giddy with longing and crazy with desire as he felt at this instant. Wondering what it would take to make her surrender...

LIBBY HAD THOUGHT if she kept it casual, kept them busy, this wouldn't happen. He wouldn't look at her in that certain way that made her feel all-woman. He wouldn't pursue her.

They wouldn't end up falling victim to the sizzling physical attraction between them.

But they had.

And now?

All she knew for certain was that when she was with Holden like this, her problems seemed a lot more manageable, her life more exciting.

He made her want to relax and move forward and play. But she wasn't a carefree girl anymore, Libby scolded herself, as the feel of his muscular frame pressed against hers sent sensations flooding through her body.

She might be *feeling* a little love-struck at the moment—probably because she had been alone so long—but it didn't make a reckless liaison any less dangerous to her heart.

She could still be hurt. Terribly.

So could he.

And that, as much as anything, was why they had to stop.

Before they did something they would both regret.

Breathlessly, she tore her mouth from his and pushed him away. "Holden. We can't."

"Sure we can." His lips closed on hers again before she could murmur another word. He kissed her long and hard, until she finally relented and kissed him back just as passionately. Again and again, until the future beckoned and her icy-cold heart began to thaw. And Libby knew this rebound romance of theirs was going to be trouble.

Big trouble.

Chapter Five

Libby was setting up the art center the library provided for the little ones when the doorbell rang the next evening. It was Holden, who, freshly showered and shaved, smelled every bit as good as he looked.

She smiled. "Hey, I didn't expect to see you tonight."

He strolled in, took off his leather bomber jacket and hung it on the coat tree next to the door. "Miss Mim assigned me as your volunteer helper for the library hours at your home."

Tingles rippled through Libby as she gazed up at him. He towered over her and made her feel petite. "Did she do that on her own or…?"

Holden's eyes twinkled at the corners. "I might have had something to do with it."

Libby's breath stalled halfway up her windpipe, reminding her just how long she had been without a man in her life.

"What did she say?"

Holden wrapped his arms around her and brought her flush against him. "She clapped me on the arm and said, 'Good luck and Godspeed.'"

Libby couldn't help it—she laughed.

A little levity was what she needed after the day she'd had.

"How are things going at the dealership?" Holden asked, brushing a brief, platonic kiss on her hairline and releasing her.

She went back to prepping for their little guests and parents, setting out coffee, cartons of juice and milk on ice, and cookies. "It was a weird day."

"How so?" Holden arranged the crayons and paper, and several sets of blocks.

Finished, Libby straightened. "Jeff Johnston was supposed to call me to get more information so his guy could do one evaluation of the property. See if it came up the same as ours. He didn't."

Holden kept his eyes on her face. "Hmm."

"Apparently, he's still running around, talking to the local ranchers, one-on-one. Trying to get a feel for the customer."

Holden closed in on her slowly. "That may not be all bad, if Johnston turns out to be a responsive business owner. People might feel a lot better about the sale. Which in turn means less pressure on you, if that is the road you're deciding to take."

If. Libby ruminated over Holden's choice of words. "Does that mean you still hope I won't sell?"

"I hope you won't leave Laramie. Not the same thing."

Did any of that have to do with them kissing on two separate occasions? Libby wondered, as a thrill ran through her.

Or the way the evening ended the night before, with the snow flurries stopping as abruptly as they had started, and them both being a little on edge…?

Not sure whether to feel guilty about any latent disloyalty to Percy, or happy that they both now knew they were capable of moving on.

Physically, anyway…

Holden cleared his throat. "What about the rest of your day?"

"Even stranger. There's a lot of tension at the dealership. Despite my reassurances that I am looking out for them, people are worried about their jobs."

"Guess that's to be expected," he rationalized.

Libby sighed and shook her head. "We were supposed to get the showroom decorated for Christmas between customers, but with staff suddenly taking a disproportionate amount of 'personal time' and the number of local ranchers coming in to chat and see if the rumors about a possible transfer of ownership are true, that didn't happen, either."

Holden perched on an arm of the sofa. "I could help you with that."

She strolled closer, studying him all the while. "Aren't you pretty busy, too?"

"During the day." He lifted his broad shoulders in a lazy shrug. "My evenings are free. And since the mini-library is only going to be open from five to seven on Monday, Wednesday and Friday evenings, that leaves tomorrow and Thursday free."

"You're sure you wouldn't mind?" Libby asked appreciatively.

His smile was slow and sexy. "Ply me with more of that delicious soup and I'll be there promptly at closing."

Libby flushed at the memory of his lips on hers. "I'll do better than that, since you're really going to have to work."

His eyes twinkled once again. "I think I'll be up to the task."

Libby was, too. That was the problem—it was difficult to be around Holden and not fantasize about all the possibilities.

"I KNOW CINDY IS ONLY six weeks old," the proud young mother told Holden seriously, shortly after the mini-library opened. "But now that she's looking around, I really think I should start reading to her."

He smiled. "It's never too soon to engender a love of reading. Let me show you where the board books are housed."

While he was busy, another half-dozen mothers came in, all doing their best to guide their excited children through the process of choosing new reading material.

"Honestly," one particularly harried young mom said, as Libby was checking out the books by hand, "sometimes I don't know what I was thinking!"

Libby knew the woman was joking about the challenge of having three rambunctious boys, roughly a year apart in age. Still...

"Was that as hard on you as it was on me?" she asked Holden after they had closed down for the night.

He gathered up the stray crayons. "I love kids."

Libby hunkered down to straighten the stacks. "You know what I mean."

"Yeah. I do," he admitted. "And being around newborn babies is particularly hard for me." His jaw tightened. "It makes me think of the baby Heidi and I lost, when she miscarried." He turned to Libby, his eyes bleak. "It was a boy, you know."

She felt his pain like a blow to the solar plexus, and she swallowed. "I didn't. Oh, Holden." She went to him and hugged him close. "I'm so sorry."

Libby had never really comforted Holden at the time. She hadn't known what to say. Now, having been through her own loss, she did. She swallowed again and drew back. "It's always going to hurt."

Grimly, Holden went back to gathering up the stray crayons. Finally, he straightened. "A lot of people tell me it will stop. Maybe not now, but—" he turned his brooding glance to hers "—when I actually do have a child."

Libby took his hand and gave it a reassuring squeeze. "I think you'll be happier when you have a child to replace the one you lost. I don't think you'll ever stop grieving. I suspect there will always be a place deep inside you that holds the sadness." She met his gaze. "A part of you that will wonder what if Heidi *hadn't* miscarried at five months along, if the baby's heart defect had been detected...and they would have had more of a chance to do something about it."

Jaw clenched, Holden nodded.

Libby gave his fingers another squeeze and let go. "Most of the time I don't think about it. I don't let myself. But tonight..." She lifted a hand and sighed. "With all those babies and toddlers..."

"I know." Holden's gaze turned compassionate. "It was hard on you, too."

Restless, she began to pace. "It reminds me that I'm thirty-two. Time is passing. I've got to get a move on if I want to have a baby of my own. And I do."

"So do I."

They looked at each other. She had an inkling what his bright idea might be. Libby flashed a weary smile. "That might be a last resort, Holden. But we're not anywhere near a last resort."

He smiled again, with the trademark McCabe mischief. "Just checking…"

Libby pushed aside the desire roaring through her, and forced herself to think rationally. "In the meantime, if you want to opt out of the volunteer assignment here, and help one of the other mini-libraries instead…?"

Holden shook his head. "My family has been after me for months now, pushing me to forge ahead, and they're right," he said with his customary determination. "I need to deal with this, Libby. Let it strengthen my resolve to have a family, instead of scaring me away."

She grinned and clapped him playfully on the shoulder. "Now you're talking."

"So…" He stepped back, all easy charm once again. "About that first date."

Persistence of this type usually annoyed Libby. But not here, and not now. Unable to help herself, she sent Holden a flirtatious glance. "We keep putting it off, don't we?"

Those blue eyes twinkled. "No time like the present."

Libby looked at her watch. They both needed a diversion. And a movie theater was a safe enough venue. "Want to see a nine-o'clock show?" she asked cheerfully.

Holden reached for his coat. "You read my mind."

THEY STOPPED BY the Dairy Barn and grabbed burgers, fries and peppermint shakes. The place was full of teenagers, so they took their meal over to the park and sat at a picnic table in the shelter. It was hard to believe they'd seen snow flurries the evening before, although none of the precipitation had stuck. But that was Texas in December—thirty-two degrees one day, sixty the next.

He ripped open a packet of ketchup. "I noticed you don't

have a Christmas tree yet. Are you planning on getting one?"

Libby ignored the romantic aura of their impromptu picnic and rummaged through the bag, looking for salt. "I've got one being delivered to the dealership for the showroom tomorrow afternoon." She frowned. "I haven't decided what to do about my house."

"What do you usually do?"

Libby's recent memories were glum. "Last year I passed. It seemed like too much effort to put one up just for me."

Holden sent her a stern look. "That's totally unacceptable."

"Uh-huh." She regarded him through narrowed lashes. "Do you have one up at your ranch house?"

He wrinkled his nose in chagrin. "Uh…"

"I thought not." She looked down her nose at him.

"Hey." He pressed a palm to his chest. "I was going to go and cut one down next weekend." He favored her with a speculative glance. "You're welcome to come with me if you want."

Libby blinked. "To a Christmas tree farm?"

"To my property. I have pine trees on the Bar M."

She dabbed her mouth with a paper napkin. "That sounds…"

His eyes lit up. "Festive?"

Libby grinned. "Like a lot of work."

His lips curled in mock exasperation. "I take it, then, you've never done it."

"Wielded an ax on a poor unsuspecting tree?" she responded, deadpan. Enjoying their banter, she sat up straight. "No, I have not."

"If it will make you feel better, I'll be sure to do all the chopping and heavy lifting, and I'll replace any trees we take with seedlings in the spring."

Libby liked the idea of that, as much as she liked hanging out with him. "You'd do that for me?"

Holden toasted her with his peppermint milk shake. "In exchange for some home-baked Christmas cookies? I sure would."

"WELL, I DIDN'T FORESEE that ending," Holden murmured later as he walked her to her front door. "A romantic comedy where the guy *doesn't* get the girl?"

Libby lingered beneath her porch light. She knew it was silly, but she'd had such a good time she didn't want the evening to end. She thrust her hands in the pockets of her red down jacket. "Kind of defeats the purpose of the movie, doesn't it? In my fantasies, I want everything to work out perfectly."

Holden's lips took on a rueful curve. He thrust his hands in his pockets, too. "I know what you mean. There's comfort in thinking that at least somewhere, some couple is deliriously happy."

Libby's mood turned wistful. "Even if they're only a fictional couple?"

"Hey." He lifted his hands amiably. "Got to take what we can get, in this life."

"How well I know that," she murmured.

They continued staring at each other.

Libby ignored what she knew was prudent and took reckless action instead. She angled her chin. "Want to come in?"

His wide shoulders relaxed. "Maybe for a minute."

She unlocked the door and decided to make this an

actual practice run, thereby giving it parameters and a purpose. "I feel as awkward as I would on a first date."

"Same here."

Silence fell. Their smiles widened and the butterflies inside her grew. Tingling with anticipation, Libby drew breath.

Holden's jaw tautened. He took her hand, suddenly reserved. "Maybe we should just say good-night," he suggested quietly.

Giving her no chance to protest, he drew her into his arms.

Libby knew he meant the kiss to be sweet—and short. She could tell by the first, closemouthed press of his lips to hers.

She also knew that wasn't going to be enough. She wanted to feel connected to him. It didn't matter that she was too caught up in the moment to think rationally. Or that taking their relationship to another level would be incredibly risky. He was so big and strong and undeniably male. It had been a long time since she had felt so beautiful and so wanted. And the kiss that had started so innocently quickly turned passionate.

Ever the gentleman, Holden started to put on the brakes and break it off.

Frustrated, Libby drew him back. "Don't go."

His hands settled on her shoulders and gripped hard. His expression was shadowed with a mixture of self-discipline and regret. "You'll hate me in the morning if I stay," he murmured grimly. "Maybe even sooner."

Libby shook her head, scarcely able to believe that what had happened before was happening again. "No, Holden. I won't," she said desperately.

Briefly, emotion flashed in his eyes, but it was gone

before Libby could decipher it. "If I could believe that..."
he said, all traces of the ardent suitor disappearing as
swiftly as they had appeared.

"For once, I just want to do what I want," Libby confessed, wanting—needing—him to see where she was
coming from. "And what I want right now, Holden, is to
make love with you."

Chapter Six

It was impossible, Holden thought, to be around Libby and not want to take her in his arms and move heaven and earth to protect her. And if this was what she needed to get through the holidays…

Tightening his grip on her, he hauled her against him and angled his head over hers. And then they were kissing in a way that felt incredibly right, in a way that demonstrated they had a lot more love and life in them than either of them had previously thought. He knew they'd be fools to throw chemistry like this away if it provided the catalyst they both needed to jump-start their personal lives.

And yet Holden knew he couldn't let things get too far out of control. He would kiss her and hold her for a few minutes and then that would be it.

But the more their mouths meshed, the more his gentlemanly intentions went by the wayside. His hands seemed to have a life of their own, and she didn't mind one bit as he found her soft curves.

Had they not lost their balance as she tried to lead him, still kissing, toward the stairs, who knew what would have happened?

But they did stumble, bumping into one of the framed photographs.

Libby managed to catch it before it crashed to the floor.

As she stood holding it in her hands, they both looked down and saw Percy's image staring up at them.

Libby drew in a sharp breath. Guilt and uncertainty flashed in her eyes, and Holden felt a sharp stab of disloyalty, too.

Her shoulder slumped. "I guess I'm not as ready to move on as I thought," she admitted with a sigh.

Was he? Holden wondered.

Especially if it meant betraying his late best friend?

Seeming to read his mind, Libby carefully put the photo on the foyer table. Her chin held high, she turned and took Holden's hand.

She wore the same look she had on her face whenever she spoke about selling the dealership and moving on with her life.

"But I'm also not willing to call a halt entirely." She paused and looked deep into his eyes. "I want to see you again." She squared her slender shoulders. "Tomorrow night okay?"

She really had changed, Holden realized in surprise. Gone were the traces of the ultra-accommodating woman his best friend had failed to appreciate.

Mesmerized by the strength of character he saw in her eyes, he curtailed his own fast-threatening-to-get-out-of-control desire, and murmured teasingly, "You sure you want to see me again so soon?" What they were feeling was already pretty intense.

"We entered into this so we can practice being part of a couple again. The point is…" Libby paused and drew a bolstering breath. "Dating after such a long drought is not going to be easy, Holden. We both knew that going into this. There are going to be glitches and missteps. Plus horrible feelings of guilt, probably. And kissing is bound to be awkward, too. So…who better to share it with than each other?"

Was she really thinking they could limit this to kisses? He was still aroused.

Quirking his lips, he retorted, "Gosh, Libby, when you put it that way…"

Completely recovered, she leaned toward him, the only clue that she'd been at all affected by their embrace being the faint imprint of her nipples against her sweater. "I'm serious, Holden. I really do want to try this again. We had a lot of fun up to now."

She had a point, he realized.

He smiled, thinking how good it had felt to share a picnic with her in the park and sit side by side in the movie theater, sharing a bucket of popcorn and some Junior Mints candy. "We did at that."

Libby perked up. "So we'll see each other again tomorrow night?"

Her enthusiasm was contagious. "I'll pick you up at seven-thirty."

She tilted her head, curious. "Where are we going to go?"

Nowhere, Holden thought sagely, anywhere near a bed.

HOLDEN ENTERED the Bar M stable just as Kurt finished examining the gestating Lady. Holden nodded at the beautiful silver mare with white feet and a dark gray mane, then turned to his cousin. "How is she doing?"

Kurt stepped out of the foaling box, vet bag in hand. "Great. Although we got the results of the blood tests back, and the results are just as you suspected they'd be. The antibodies are up significantly."

Which meant they were facing hemolytic disease in the foal, Holden thought.

Kurt continued casually, "You know what to do, so there shouldn't be any problem, but if you run into difficulty, just call me."

He nodded. "Sure thing."

His cousin joined him in the aisle. "You still want me to look at the foal that was born this morning?"

Holden nodded and he led the way. "Mind if I ask you a question?"

"Go ahead." Kurt carried his veterinary bag into the stall. Exhausted from the rigors of giving birth, the big bay mare was lying on her side in the straw. Her colt was cuddled up next to her tummy.

"You're happily married," Holden remarked, as he stepped in to gently help the wobbly-legged colt to his feet.

"I certainly am, and I don't mind saying, it's great." Kurt checked the foal's limbs and evaluated the flexor and extensor tendons. "Had I known just *how* great, I would have—"

He stopped abruptly, the way blissfully married folks always did when they realized they'd put their foot in it.

"It's okay," Holden remarked, looking forward to the day he wasn't known as a divorced rancher who'd had his heart broken. "I know I failed big-time at the marriage business, first time around." Because if he hadn't, he and Heidi would have stayed together after the loss of their baby.

"Still—" Kurt paused to listen to the colt's heart and lungs "—I didn't have to rub it in."

"It's fact. I'm dealing with it. Moving on."

Kurt looked up in surprise, as Holden plunged on.

"Which brings me back to my question. How would you feel if something happened to you…?"

Kurt peered at the foal's gums. "Meaning I go to the big tent in the sky?"

He nodded. "And another guy came along and put a move on Paige?"

His cousin removed a thermometer from his bag. "I don't think I would feel anything in that scenario, because I'd be dead."

Holden brushed off the joke. "I'm serious."

"That's what worries me." Kurt stripped off the first pair of gloves, donned another and drew blood for the lab work. Then he studied Holden. "This is about Libby Lowell, isn't it?"

"I promised Percy I would look after Libby if anything ever happened to him."

"And you have." Kurt gave the antibiotic and tetanus injections. "We all know that."

"I asked to be her rebound guy. And she offered to be my rebound woman."

Kurt examined the colt's navel stump. "Did you agree?"

Hell, yes. Out loud, Holden said rhetorically, "What do you think?"

"Only now you're having second thoughts," Kurt guessed, leading the infant colt to its mama to suckle.

"It sounded easy enough at the outset," Holden confided as the foal began to nurse. "Libby and I planned to date each other through the holidays—to sort of get our sea legs back. And then that would be it. We would go our separate ways, move on to real relationships."

The other man nodded approvingly at the foal's vigor, before turning back. "So what's the problem?"

"We're just a couple days into our grand plan," he confessed, as they stepped out of the stall. "And I'm not sure we can keep our emotions in check."

Kurt removed the stethoscope from around his neck. "What are we talking here…physical attraction?"

"And guilt—that this is not what Percy had in mind when he asked me to take care of Libby."

Kurt packed up his vet bag. "He wanted Libby to be happy. He wanted her to be safe."

"Yeah?" Holden started out of the barn.

His cousin fished in his pocket for his keys. "He probably also wanted her to be loved."

Holden's mood remained skeptical. "By his best friend?"

Kurt lingered next to his pickup truck and thought a moment. "I don't think jealousy exists in heaven. I think all those negative emotions are filtered out. They'd have to be, for anyone to have eternal peace."

"You've got a point there," Holden said quietly at last.

Kurt tossed his gear in the cab. "You and Libby, on the other hand, are still here on earth. So you're going to have the whole gamut of emotions to deal with, whether this works out the way you two envisioned or not."

Holden turned his face into the wind, eyeing up the gray clouds overhead. Christmas and New Year's would be here sooner than they thought. And with that, the end of his arrangement with Libby. "So what are you saying? It's only going to get worse?"

"No clue. The only thing I do know—" Kurt slapped him companionably on the back and flashed an encouraging grin "—is that you, my friend, are in deep."

"LIBBY?" VINCE HUNT ASKED shortly after the dealership closed for the day. "Got a minute? We all have something we'd like to say to you."

Her nerves jangling, Libby walked out into the showroom, where all her employees were gathered. She was pleased to see the staff had gotten together and decorated the showroom for Christmas, as tradition required, making Holden's help that evening unnecessary.

The head of financial services continued, "We're sorry about the way we confronted you the other day. Since then, we've all had the opportunity to sit down with Jeff Johnston individually."

So that was what had been going on….

Speaking for the service department, Manny Pierce chimed in, "He let us know that he really takes care of his employees, and he is planning to run the business on the same model Southwest Airlines uses."

This was news. "You'd each own a small part of the company through profit sharing?" Libby asked in surprise.

Heads bobbed happily.

Lucia Gordon smiled. "He's really focused on building each business he owns into a cohesive team. Plus he said he would give us all written contracts and guaranteed salaries and bonuses for the next five years."

"After meeting with him one-on-one, we realize he's a decent guy," Swifty Mortimer said. "So we're all okay with it now."

"Not that we want to see you go," Manny Pierce hastened to add. "But…we understand."

Libby was so shocked she didn't know what to say. Finally, she managed to thank everyone for their support.

"And one more thing," the receptionist said, handing Libby a slip of paper. "This call came in while you were with that last customer."

Holden's name was scrawled across the top. The message beneath read: "Sorry about tonight. Rain check?"

Not sure what that meant, Libby worked to keep her expression inscrutable. "That's it?"

Lucia shrugged. "He sounded like he was in a hurry."

"Okay, thanks."

Libby went into her office and tried to reach Holden, both on his cell phone and on the ranch line.

There was no answer either place.

Which meant what? she wondered, beginning to feel a little upset. Had he learned the dealership had already been decorated and changed his mind about spending time with her tonight? Or was it more than that?

Realizing there was only one way to find out, Libby got in her car and drove out to the Bar M ranch. She hadn't been out there in almost two years, and she was surprised to see how much had changed.

There were now countless pastures and four large stables, a barn and the original fieldstone ranch house with the steeply pitched roof.

Holden's pickup was parked in the drive. Light spilled from one of the buildings, and she headed that way. Holden was inside, kneeling next to a newborn foal, slipping a muzzle over its head.

He looked up as Libby slipped into the stall.

"Hi," she said softly, amazed as always at the fragility and wonder of new life.

She knelt down beside the foal, which was the spitting image of its mama—silver body, dark gray mane, white feet.

Holden flashed her a sexy smile. "I guess you got my message."

"Yeah." He was really in his element.

Wishing she'd thought to change into jeans and boots, or at least brought some with her, Libby hunkered down beside him, being careful not to get the goo from the birth on any of her nice work clothes. "What are you doing?"

Holden went to the cooler in the corner and brought out a bottle of what looked like formula. "Prenatal tests determined this foal has hemolytic disease. In other words, there was a blood group incompatibility between the dam and the sire. Antibodies are produced during pregnancy that, if ingested by the foal, would destroy her red blood cells."

Admiring Holden's competence, Libby asked, "Sort of like Rh disease in humans?"

"Right." He shook the bottle, making sure its contents were mixed. "Although in babies, it's a little more complicated. With horses, all we have to do to keep the foal from harm is substitute compatible colostrum for the first thirty-six hours, and make sure Willow here doesn't nurse and ingest any of Lady's."

"Hence the muzzle," Libby guessed.

"I'll milk the mother six times a day and discard her colostrum, to prevent any from being transferred to the foal, and feed Willow by hand. Then she'll nurse at her mother's side, as per usual."

"Wow. You really know your stuff."

He grinned. "Breeding and training quarter horses is my profession."

And, Libby thought admiringly, he did it very well.

"Want to help with the first feeding?"

Was he kidding? "Love to," Libby said.

Holden produced the bottle for the newborn and a wooden bench for Libby to sit on. With gentle hands, he undid the muzzle and helped them get situated, with Willow braced and supported by Libby's knees.

Looking content but exhausted, the mama horse lay on her side, watching.

As the sleek little foal began to suck on the bottle, Libby was filled with tenderness. She slanted Holden an appreciative glance. "No wonder you couldn't make our date."

"Sorry I couldn't leave a more detailed message. I just figured I would call you later. I didn't expect you to drive all the way out here." Holden paused to study her, his expression maddeningly inscrutable. "Why *did* you drive all the way out here?"

Libby flushed and struggled to keep her guard up. Before her heart went from foolishly wishing for more than a rebound-dating experience with Holden, to being completely vulnerable.

She forced herself to glance away from him. "I tried calling—there was no answer."

He braced his hands on his hips, his eyes guarded now. "Did you think I'd changed my mind about helping you and I was standing you up?"

Libby drew a breath, reassuring herself that even after the hot intensity of their kisses, they were in no real danger of actually hooking up. They were both much too sensible for that. She gestured with her free hand. "First of all, the decorating has been done today by LRE staff. And, after last night…"

Holden's jaw set with McCabe resolve. "We were smart to stop when we did. Continuing after the picture fell… well, that would have been really awkward."

It certainly had broken the mood.

Libby gave a sigh of relief. "So it's not just me."

"It's not just you." An indecipherable emotion crossed his face.

As they headed for the exit half an hour later, when

the foal had been fed, Holden put a hand on the small of Libby's back and surveyed her closely. "Since you're here and things are calm in the barn for now…want to come inside with me?"

She ignored the heat radiating from his palm. "Sure."

Together, they crossed the yard and walked into the two-story fieldstone ranch house.

Unlike her home, where photos of Percy and his family abounded, Holden's house had been wiped clean of any memory of Heidi and their marriage. But then that was to be expected, since they were divorced. As she looked around, Libby couldn't help but wonder if that was a healthier way to live, in the wake of loss….

Casually, Holden advised, "Make yourself at home. I'm going to shower. After that, maybe we can rustle up some dinner."

Left alone, Libby wandered into the kitchen, switched on the lights and got her second surprise of the evening.

Chapter Seven

"What's all this?"

The icy note in Libby's voice stopped Holden in his tracks.

He ran a hand through his freshly shampooed hair and followed her gaze to the stacks of paperwork on his kitchen table. Too late, he realized he probably should have told her about this when she first arrived at the ranch.

He'd certainly meant to mention it.

Had she not showed up so unexpectedly and looked so damn gorgeous in tailored black slacks and an evergreen wool blazer, he probably would have told her. Instead, all he'd been able to focus on was how soft and silky her hair looked, falling about her shoulders.

Holden edged closer, taking in the agitated color in her sculpted cheeks and the stormy set of her luscious lips. Calmly, he brought her up to speed. "Jeff Johnston stopped by earlier today. He gave me the full sales pitch. Told me how good this would be for you."

She raised her chin. "Bottom line?"

Okay, so she was ticked off at him. Holden matched her contentious tone. "He wanted me to use my influence with you to try and get you to sell to him."

She released a short, bitter laugh. "And you said?"

"That you're a very intelligent woman who likes to make up her own mind. I also warned him that tactics like this were not likely to put him in your good graces."

Libby watched him get the coffeemaker out. "You can say that again."

Holden poured coffee grounds into the paper filter. "I'm not the only rancher he's visited. He's been making the rounds of all your customers."

"And my employees." Frowning, Libby told Holden about the meeting she'd had with her staff before she had come over to see him.

Holden added water and switched on the machine. "How do you feel about that?"

"Honestly?" She leaned against the counter and rubbed the toe of her suede pump across the wide-plank oak floor. "I don't know what to think." She bit her lip. "He seems to have convinced everyone that he would do one heck of a lot better job running the dealership than I have."

"And that hurts," Holden guessed, wrapping a consoling arm about her shoulders.

Libby settled into the curve of his arm in a drift of cinnamon perfume. "I thought I had done a good job." She shook her head. "Sales are on par with what Percy—and his parents—managed. I've given everyone bonuses and cost-of-living raises."

"I know they all appreciate that."

"Yeah." Libby fell silent.

"I thought this was what you wanted."

"So did I," she admitted.

Sensing there was more, he waited.

She ran her hands through her hair, then turned to look up at him. "I didn't expect to get what I wished for so quickly." She stepped back slightly so they were no longer touching.

Holden pushed aside the need to pull her into his arms and kiss her again. "Has Johnston come in with a number yet?" he asked.

"No." Libby sighed. "But given how determined he is to make the deal, I can't imagine he would offer anything insulting."

"You can still turn him down." *Stay here in Laramie.* "Keep the business in the family, so to speak."

Regret pinched the corners of her mouth. "Actually, Holden," she said softly, "I can't."

LIBBY COULD TELL by the way Holden was looking at her that she was acting like a flighty woman unable to make up her mind.

She couldn't help it. Her emotions were a mess. And who better to hear why than the man who had already seen her at her worst, and thought no less of her?

"I still feel bad about selling, because even though the Lowell name will be on the dealership, there'll be no one from the family actually involved in running the business."

He got two mugs from the cupboard. "And that ends three generations of tradition."

Libby frowned. "That's not what Percy or his parents would have wanted."

Holden filled the mugs with the fragrant brew. "You're right." He paused to pass her one. "As much as Percy sometimes resented being handed a career, he was proud of what his family had built."

Libby sipped the hot, delicious coffee. "I'm proud of it, too. And now I'm on the brink of ending that."

Holden took her elbow and led her to the living room.

"Have you thought about keeping the dealership yourself and just hiring someone else to run the day-to-day operations?"

She settled on the handsome leather sofa. "I'd still have to be involved on some level. And that would keep me from moving on to a life of my choosing."

"Which would be where?" he asked as he sat down beside her.

Libby turned toward him. "I don't know that, either. I was thinking Austin, because I grew up there, but most of my friends have moved away." She drew a bracing breath. Became way too aware of the soapy clean scent of his hair and skin.

Pushing aside a mental image of Holden in the shower, she forged on. "Would being there just remind me of losing Aunt Ida?"

Compassion shone in his blue eyes.

Libby swallowed. "I could certainly relocate to Dallas or Houston. There would be plenty of opportunity for whatever I might choose to do with my life."

"But no family or friends."

She traced the UT insignia on the coffee mug. "I don't have family anywhere."

Holden lifted his mug to his lips. "That will change."

She met his eyes and didn't look away. "Will it?" she countered softly, feeling a little depressed again, like the hero in *A Charlie Brown Christmas*. "I don't seem to have much luck in that department."

Holden put his coffee aside. "I know you feel unattached, Libby. Sometimes I feel that way, too."

She set her mug down in turn. "But you have all those McCabes."

He took her hand in his and turned it palm up. "And no wife or kids of my own."

Libby couldn't imagine how anyone as kind, handsome and smart as Holden would ever go through his entire life alone. "That will change."

He traced her life line with his index finger. "That's what everyone says."

And yet he remained skeptical.

"Once we start dating again, actively looking, we'll find what we want," Libby declared.

She knew what *she* wanted. Someone just like Holden.

He let go of her hand and studied her. "You really think so?"

"We have to." Restlessly, she got to her feet and paced over to the window, where she looked out at the dark night. "Because I can't go on this way, Holden." Her voice caught. "I can't live the rest of my life without family ties."

He rose and walked toward her, all empathetic male. "You could become an honorary McCabe."

Libby knew Holden wanted her to have everything she would have if her husband hadn't died, but this was getting ridiculous. "You really are taking this 'a life for a life' thing too far."

One corner of his mouth quirked. "What's wrong with having a place to go on every holiday?" he challenged, his gaze roving her face. "A group to hang out with?"

"How would your parents feel about that?" Libby retorted.

He shrugged and slid his hands into the back pockets of his jeans. "They *want* me bringing a new woman into the tribe."

"As your wife," she pointed out.

He tilted his head to one side. "You're my girlfriend.

Well, practice girlfriend." Mischief glimmered in his expression. "In the loosest sense of the word."

Libby ignored the tingling sensation in her middle. "It doesn't matter how serious we are. Or aren't." She couldn't bear to experience anything that only invited more loss, as this eventually would.

Holden clearly felt otherwise.

"Girlfriends get invited to family events," he stated sagely. "Friends, too, for that matter."

Libby rolled her eyes. "Friends who have no place to go."

Holden put his hands on her shoulders. "I'm serious, Libby." He waited until she looked him in the eye. "There is no reason for you to spend this Christmas and New Year's or any other alone." His grip tightened protectively. "I want you to spend it with me and my family, and I'm not taking no for an answer."

Misery warred with the building excitement within her, but Libby forced herself to be practical. "You're going to have to," she retorted.

He dropped his hands, stepped back. "Why?"

"Because, Holden, I know what it's like to start out as one thing—a beloved niece, a girlfriend, a wife—and then turn into more of a liability than either of us could ever imagine. I don't want to be that again. Not for you. And certainly," she finished heavily, "not for your entire family."

LIBBY WAS JUST GETTING ready to leave for work the next morning when the doorbell rang.

Thinking it might be Holden—whom she'd parted with awkwardly the evening before—she went to answer the door and found Holden's mother there.

"I hope you don't mind my dropping in this way," Greta said. She had a coffee shop bag in one hand, a cardboard beverage holder in the other.

Libby ushered the elegant older woman inside. As usual, Greta's curly silver-blond hair was impeccably coiffed. She had on a trim denim shirtdress and a festive green Christmas cardigan that complemented the bright smile on her face.

"Holden said you liked vanilla lattes and cranberry scones, so that's what I brought," she said warmly.

Libby took her coat, then led her into the formal dining room. "I do. Thank you."

They chatted a moment about the weather, and the thus far fruitless efforts to get the county officials to fund repairs on the library.

"But I know you didn't come over here at eight-thirty in the morning just to discuss this," Libby said. "What's on your mind?"

Greta sipped her latte. "I understand you and my son are dating."

"Very casually," she replied.

"So you don't see this leading anywhere...?"

In her wildest dreams? Libby clamped down on the fantasies their two kisses had inspired. If she was smart, she would not allow herself to go there.

"Realistically? I don't see how it could," she finally replied.

Greta nodded. "Holden told me as much, too."

Disappointment spiraled through Libby. That was the problem with even casual dating, she thought. It could still leave you hurt and wanting—needing—more. Especially at this time of year...

"Holden said he invited you to spend the holidays with us."

And not just one Christmas and New Year, but all the holidays from here on out.

Libby worked to contain her lingering sadness. "That's right. He did."

"And?" Curiosity filled his mother's eyes.

Libby reminded herself that leaving Laramie was the only way she would ever be able to build a life for herself, and get everything she wanted, like a husband and children. "I know Holden's heart was in the right place, that he feels for me because I have no family of my own left. But…"

When she couldn't go on, Holden's mom filled in the rest. "You think assuaging guilt and making good on a deathbed promise to your late husband aren't reason enough to bring anyone into the family, even unofficially."

Leave it to her to cut straight to the chase.

Libby sighed, relieved to be able to be forthright, too. "It sounds like a good solution now. And it probably would make me feel less alone during the holiday season."

"But…" the older woman prompted.

Libby grimaced. "But what happens when the rebound relationship Holden and I have embarked on ends, and he's with someone else?" She shrugged and pushed the unpleasant thought away. "I can't see his next girlfriend being comfortable having his old girlfriend—even a decidedly platonic one—at family gatherings. Can you?"

Greta relaxed. "To be honest, I don't see that as a problem. Our family has grown so much and our get-togethers have gotten so large…. Plus, by the time that happens, you might very well have your own special someone to bring with you, too. Or you might be at your new love's family gathering instead of ours."

Oddly enough, Libby did not see that as a comfort, either. Although it should be....

Greta continued gently, "What I do see as a continuing difficulty is the confusion Holden feels about *how* he is supposed to look after you in Percy's absence. Right now, the responsibility is all on his shoulders. Clearly, the obligation is weighing on him."

Libby began to see where this was going. "But that might change if he felt others were looking after me, too." In the loving, caring, all-inclusive way that the McCabes were famous for...

His mom nodded. "If you became part of the McCabe tribe, you'd have any number of people you could call on, at any time, to help and support you in any way you needed."

The burden would be lifted from Holden's heart.

Finally seeing a way out of the morass they'd found themselves in for two long years, Libby concluded, "Reassured, Holden would be able to move on with his life. He would be able to be happy again."

Greta smiled. "You both would."

"I THOUGHT LIBBY WAS coming with you tonight," Shane McCabe said when Holden arrived at the Annie's Homemade food-testing facility.

Because the family had a lot to accomplish that evening, and dozens of McCabes to do it, the gathering was being held in his aunt Annie's place of business. The large space was outfitted with dozens of picnic tables and still had plenty of open floor. Outside, where most of the men were at the moment, trucks were being unloaded, Christmas trees trimmed, spare greenery carried inside.

Trying not to be disappointed that another of their "dates" had taken a detour, Holden pulled on his leather work gloves and told his dad, "Scheduling conflict. I've got a foal that still needs hand-feeding. Libby had library hours at her home. So she's meeting me here."

A fact that had deprived him of picking her up and driving her in his truck, like a real date, Holden mused in disappointment.

Shane set a Christmas tree upside down. "How is the sale of her business going?"

Wade and Travis joined them and began trimming trees, too.

Holden picked up a small handsaw, appropriate for the job. "As far as I know, she's getting everything she is asking for from Jeff Johnston."

Holden's dad and two brothers stopped what they were doing and exchanged surprised looks.

Holden exhaled, glad to have the three accomplished businessmen to use as a sounding board. "Yeah, I know. Generally, when something seems too good to be true, it is. And whether she wants to come right out and admit it or not, Libby intuits that, too."

Silence fell. The tree trimming and bundling resumed.

Holden wrapped a net around a spruce ready for transport to the Kiwanis Club's holiday lot. "I've done some research, checked into Johnston's other acquisitions. He seems to have the golden touch when it comes to expanding a business and taking it onto the internet. Neither Libby nor I have been able to find any formal complaints lodged against him that would indicate he's done anything even borderline unethical or illegal."

"And yet—" Shane added another trimmed tree to the

pile "—something about this situation just doesn't sit right, does it?"

"I don't like the way he's gone behind Libby's back, talking to all her employees, promising them the moon so they'll get on board with the sale," Holden admitted.

Travis sawed the lower limbs off a tree. "Not to mention chatting up all the ranchers in the area, to make them believe he would do a much better job of meeting our needs than Libby ever could."

"Intense competition in the business world is expected," Wade pointed out as he piled the shorn strips of greenery onto a wheeled cart. He shook his head in mute disapproval. "Stabbing rivals in the back is not."

Which in a way, Holden thought, was exactly what Johnston was currently doing. *If* his intentions were of the nasty, competitive ilk...

Holden struggled to be objective, but it wasn't easy when Libby's well-being was at stake. "I'm trying to be fair. To consider whether Johnston is simply being proactive—and attempting to reassure everyone, in advance, that his intentions are as honorable as he professes. Or—" he grimaced, considering the alternative "—is Johnston's behavior an indication that he is a hell of a lot more cutthroat than we know, and Libby really needs to beware?"

Another concerned silence fell.

"What do you want us to do?" Shane asked.

Wade was a multimillionaire investor, his uncle Travis and his dad prominent members of all the ranching associations in the state. Among the three of them, Holden knew they had a powerful, knowledgeable network of acquaintances. "Use your connections. Ask around. See if there's anything you can find out about Johnston that might be a red flag."

His dad guessed the rest. "And while we're at it, don't mention to Libby what we're doing."

Holden ignored the faint hint of disapproval coming from all three older men. Determined to keep his promise and watch over Libby, whether she liked it or not, he said drily, "You may have heard she doesn't like being protected."

"We'll do what you ask, son," Shane promised with the understanding of a man who had been happily married for over thirty-five years. "But don't be surprised if Libby doesn't thank you for it."

Chapter Eight

"If I didn't know better, I would think I just walked into Santa's Workshop," Libby teased, when she finally met up with Holden and he escorted her inside the Annie's Homemade testing facility.

The McCabes gathering was a beehive of activity that included every conceivable yuletide activity. Wreaths were being made for the Kiwanis Club. Gift baskets assembled for the Blue Santa organization. Stockings sewed for the Community Chapel bazaar.

Everywhere Libby and Holden looked, there were children playing, adults laughing. Christmas carols resonated in the background, adding to the festive mood, and the sweet smell of sugar cookies scented the air.

Recognizing them immediately, Paige and Kurt's two-year-old triplets rushed over to greet them. They looked adorable in red velvet dresses, white tights and cute black boots with knit uppers. Arms outstretched, the little girls shouted, "Holden! Libby!"

Grinning, Holden scooped up Lori and Lucille. Libby picked up Lindsay. Dark curls bouncing, cherubic faces grinning blissfully, the toddlers chatted away, talking in two- or three-word sentences.

"So Santa is coming?" Libby asked, a wave of maternal

contentment flowing through her as she cradled the little one in her arms.

All three girls nodded enthusiastically.

Looking as happy as she felt, Holden asked, "Are you going to bake cookies for him?"

There were more nods, along with shouts of "cookies!"

The notion planted, the girls wiggled out of their arms and raced over to the buffet tables, where their mom was helping Annie McCabe replenish the plates of refreshments for the volunteers.

Paige and Annie waved at them before turning to give the triplets the cookies they were asking for.

Holden's mother welcomed Libby and him with warm hugs. "Thanks for coming," she said with a beleaguered sigh, running a hand through her curls. "As you can see, we need all the help we can get. Do you want to eat or work first?"

"Work," Holden and Libby decided in unison.

Greta gave them a considering glance. "Okay, then. I'll put you right to work. We have a lot of toys that were donated for the children's home in San Angelo that need to be wrapped, so I'll put you on that, Libby. Holden, we have some saddles that are going to the boys' ranch in Libertyville, that need to be cleaned and reconditioned... so I'll leave that to you."

"Why so much all at once?" he asked.

It was usually a little crazy this time of year, but not *this* chaotic... And why were things being done in such a way that would keep the men and woman largely separated this evening? he wondered in frustration. Why couldn't his mother have set things up so he could be by Libby's side throughout the evening?

Not that Libby looked all that distressed about being left on her own…

Oblivious to the disgruntled nature of his thoughts, Greta answered, "Everyone in the family wants to get together. We all want to help the community. And like every year, it seems all the civic and charitable organizations want everything done at once."

"I know what you mean," Libby sympathized. "Every weekend in December you have to choose where you're going to go, who you're going to help. And with the library in flux this year, too…"

"A lot of events are held simultaneously," Holden noted.

Her mind already searching for a solution to the problem, Libby murmured, "It'd be nice if they could coordinate it so more people could participate in all the events."

"Wouldn't it?" Greta agreed wistfully, looking hopeful that Libby's idea would eventually see the light of day. "In the meantime, Holden, the saddles are out in one of the barns. Your dad can direct you. And, Libby…right this way…"

Three hours later, the tasks were completed, gifts stored or dispersed, sleepy children carried out.

Disappointed that they hadn't spent more time together—hadn't even been able to grab a bite at the same time—Holden walked Libby out to her car. He knew it was late. Nearly eleven. But he still wanted to spend time with her. The kind they would have if they'd been on an actual date.

"Want to come by my ranch and see the foal? It's been thirty-six hours since she was born, so I can remove the muzzle and let Willow have her first feeding with her mama."

An event that for Holden was always a thrill, no matter how many horses he had bred and ushered into the world.

Luckily for him, Libby did not even hesitate. "I'll meet you there."

"I CAN'T BELIEVE HOW MUCH stronger she seems," Libby murmured as Holden removed the muzzle.

They watched the foal and mare nuzzle each other in the warm and cozy straw-lined stall before getting down to the business of nursing.

Holden tenderly stroked the mother and her newborn, then paused to adjust the Velcro straps on the foal's warming blanket. Satisfied that all was as it should be, he stepped back.

Admiring how gentle he was with the horses, and how much they seemed to love him, Libby murmured, "Willow is certainly happy to be able to nurse at her mama's side." You could practically feel the bliss radiating from them both.

Holden moved closer to Libby and folded his arms. "One of the best things about being in the horse-breeding business is the constant reminder of the wonder and the fragility of life."

She turned toward him, her shoulder brushing his in the process. From this angle, his profile was even more rugged, his expression poignantly tender. She couldn't help but think what a good father he would be.

"Although," Holden added, "as in most professions, there are certainly days I don't enjoy."

Inhaling the scents of saddle soap and leather clinging to his skin, she said, "It must be really hard on you when things go wrong."

A pained expression crossed his face. "It is," he admitted ruefully.

Libby thought about the child he had lost to miscarriage, and the child she had wanted and never been blessed with.

The intimacy of the moment, coupled with the understanding in his eyes, prompted her to confess, "Tonight was hard, too."

Holden swung around to face her. "Being around so much of my family?" he asked. "'Cause I know we McCabes can be overwhelming, especially en masse...."

Libby held up a hand. "No. Joining the gathering tonight was the easy part. Everyone made me feel so welcome, especially your mom and dad." Being part of a family again, even unofficially, had felt good. "It was seeing all your cousins and siblings, the people our age, who are happily married and have kids." She paused to look into Holden's eyes. "They were all so happy. Enjoying the holiday season so much!"

He eased out of the stall and held the door for her.

Smiling in appreciation, Libby joined him in the cement aisleway. As they headed toward the barn exit, Holden gave her a fond glance and mused, "That makes you feel like you're missing out."

They shut the door to the heated barn and walked across the lawn, shivering in the wintry air. Impulsively, Libby slipped her hand in Holden's and eased closer to his body heat. It was late. Almost midnight. But she had no wish to go home.

Bypassing her car, she asked curiously, "Doesn't it do the same to you?"

Looking pleased she had decided to stay awhile longer, he led the way into the house. "Of course. Especially at

Christmas, but I try not to dwell on it." He switched on lights in the foyer, living room and kitchen.

"The fact is," he continued pragmatically, "there are a lot of happy people our age who are way ahead of us when it comes to establishing their own families. But there's really not much either of us can do to catch up."

Unable to help herself, Libby teased, "Besides start dating again?" Which they were doing, albeit not very well, thus far.

Holden shook his head. "To create the chemistry necessary for the foundation of any enduring relationship. Bottom line, the spark between a man and a woman is either there—or it's not."

And it was there with the two of them. How well she knew that. So the question was…what were they waiting for?

HOLDEN KNEW THE INSTANT the mood changed. Her lips parted ever so slightly. Her irises darkened. Her whole body leaned toward him.

Yet even as desire surged within him, the memory of their last tryst returned. He took her face in his hands. "If you don't want me to kiss you again…" he warned hoarsely.

Libby's hands moved from his chest to his shoulders, before clasping behind his neck. She rose on tiptoe, her breasts brushing against his pecs. "That's just it, Holden," she whispered back. "I do."

Blood thundered through his veins as he threaded his fingers through her hair, then lowered his mouth to hers. "Then heaven help us both," he growled. "Because that's what I want, too."

It didn't matter that their "dating" was supposed to be

nothing more than a means to an end, a way to get them back into the habit of going out with others. Something happened when they were together. And it was more than hormones. More than grief or guilt or the need to give her a reason to live her life fully again.

What they had together was no longer obligation, Holden thought. It was…magic. It fulfilled a need that was deeper and more powerful than anything he had ever known.

And he sensed, from the hot, passionate way she was clinging to him and returning his kisses, that she felt the fierce pull of their attraction, too.

LIBBY HAD KNOWN it was dangerous to go back to Holden's ranch tonight. More risky still to step inside the house with him, this late, with nothing on her mind except quelling the deep-seated loneliness she had been feeling.

She told herself to go with the physical part of the experience and keep her emotions safely in check.

Yet as his hard body pressed against hers, and his fingers brushed along her jaw, her skin heated and her pulse fluttered wildly. He tasted so good, so incredibly male. She moaned as his lips dominated hers and he invaded her mouth with his tongue. He kissed her so thoroughly he took her breath away, until she whimpered softly and clung to him, every inch of her tingling with need.

And he wanted her, too—she could feel it in the hardness of his body. And that left her aching and vulnerable, wanting desperately to see where lovemaking with him would lead. Despite her decision to remain unaffected, yearnings she had pushed aside came rushing to the fore. It had been so long since she had felt so feminine or desired.

Never had she been kissed and touched so gently and so masterfully.

Filled with abandon, she whispered, "Let's go upstairs."

"I'm all for that." Tucking an arm beneath her knees, Holden carried her to the second floor and down the hall to the master bedroom.

Her heart raced as he set her down.

Afraid she might do something really foolish—like fall head over heels in love with him—if she didn't set some parameters, Libby cautioned, "Just so we're straight. We're merely..."

Once again, he read her mind. "Practicing here?"

"Yes."

What a relief he understood that because of their previous connections, this could never go anywhere beyond the here and now.

Holden unbuttoned her blouse and kissed her collarbone. "I am a little rusty."

Relaxing, Libby unbuttoned his shirt, too. Tugged it from the waistband of his jeans. Damn, but he had a nice chest. Solid, warm, with satin skin and flat male nipples buried in the mat of crisp dark hair. Broad, muscular shoulders, too. She caressed it all with her fingertips. "Then that makes two of us."

He bared her to her waist and let his glance drift over her, taking in her soft curves and jutting nipples. Exploring her breasts with his mouth, he murmured, "I'm thinking it will all come back to us."

And come back to them it did.

They undressed each other at leisure, exploring as they went, then stretched out next to each other on the bed. Murmuring in pleasure, he kissed his way down her body.

When she arched her spine, moving against him, he shuddered, too.

"I want you now," Libby breathed, drawing him upward once again.

Together, they sheathed him. Trembling, impatient, she opened herself to his possession. Holden caught her by the hips, lifted her, and then they were one. Overcome with sensation, shuddering with pleasure...

"You feel so good," he whispered.

So right, Libby thought, rising up to meet him. Her body closed around him, their coupling as honest and exciting as she had hoped it would be.

"So do you..."

Reveling in the freedom to go after exactly what she wanted—when she wanted it—she wrapped her arms and legs around him, drawing him as deep inside her as he could go. Making him aware of every soft inch of her, every need. And she was just as clued in to him. As he dived deep, she sighed and gasped in surrender. Then all reason fled, and they were lost in the passion—lost in each other—and the sweet, searing satisfaction.

"WE NEED MORE ground rules."

Those weren't the words Holden expected to hear after making hot, wild, incredible love. He sat up in bed, watching Libby rise and begin to dress.

He had always known she had a good body. However, he had never expected her to be this beautiful, naked. Her peachy skin was silky and smooth, her feminine curves gorgeous.

He eyed the mussed strands of honey-blond hair framing her face and falling across her slender shoulders as she buttoned up her blouse.

"Rules for this?" Holden asked, admiring the view from where he sat.

Libby tugged on her jeans. "Absolutely!"

Holden slanted her a cajoling grin. "Some things are better left spontaneous."

She wrinkled her nose at him and circled the bed. Snatching her socks off the floor, she sat down next to him to tug them on.

Her feet, Holden noted, were as stunningly attractive as the rest of her. His eyes roved over her slim ankles, nicely formed arches and heels, and those dainty toes gleaming with hot-pink nail polish.

"In normal cases, I would agree." Libby leaned forward to snag her boots. Soft blue denim molded her derriere and thighs.

Grabbing hold of a boot with both hands, she tugged it on, then changed legs and donned the other. Finished, she rose to her feet and whirled to face him. "But this isn't the usual situation...."

Figuring this argument could go on for a while, Holden decided to get comfortable. He reclined on one side, his head propped up on his hand. "I agree," he said lazily, a little irked to find Libby pretending the two of them hadn't just enjoyed really outstanding lovemaking—the best of *his* life, anyway!

Locking eyes with her, he stated firmly, "It's better."

Color flooded her cheeks. "Because there are no strings?"

"No expectations," he qualified, determined to hold on to what they had, whether she cooperated or not.

Her brow furrowed quizzically.

"You keep saying you don't want to be anyone else's ball

and chain," he pointed out with as much patience—and common sense—as he could summon.

Libby ran both hands over her hair, restoring order to the sensually mussed strands as best she could. "Never mind your responsibility—out of grief and guilt."

Holden surveyed her head to toe before returning with laser accuracy to her green eyes. "So isn't it better if we forget trying to plan ahead and just let what's bound to occur happen all on its own?"

Chapter Nine

It was a good question, Libby thought, and one she would have preferred not to have to answer.

"Look, Holden, I enjoyed making love with you."

He pulled back the sheet and stood. "And I really enjoyed making love with *you*."

Libby swallowed at the sight of all that masculinity. She tried not to think about the sizzling sexual promise of his body joining with hers. Forgetting for a moment how good it had felt to be clasped in his arms, she continued sternly, "But sex wasn't part of our rebound-romance agreement."

He grinned, striding toward her in all that naked glory. Stopping just short of her, he reached down and snagged his boxer briefs. Slid in one leg, then the other. "I agree." He brought the gray jersey up his rock-hard thighs to his waist, a move that did nothing to disguise his eagerness to make love with her again. "It's a totally separate clause in the implied contract between us."

Libby propped her hands on her hips and locked eyes with him once again. "One we haven't negotiated," she pointed out.

"Until now."

Was she ready for this?

She inhaled a jerky breath. Put up a staying palm. "Holden…"

Disappointment flared in his eyes. "I'm guessing you need time to think about it."

Libby stiffened. "We both do."

He gave her a look that indicated this was not the case for him. "You're pulling away," he said, his eyes darkening.

"It might be good for both of us to take a day or two to clear our heads," she volunteered softly.

"I disagree." Frown lines bracketed his sensual lips. "I see nothing to be gained by losing momentum. Unless—" he came a step closer, his assessing glance roving over her upturned face "—that's what you're counting on?" He caught her wrist and lifted it to his lips. "To get us both to a place where we can't just pick up again?"

Skin tingling, she pulled away. "I can't believe you just said that to me."

He didn't back down. "You'd prefer I be my usual gallant self?"

Libby struggled to maintain her composure in the face of all that masculine determination. "Well, yes," she admitted.

"Sorry." He seduced her with his deep, sexy voice. "For once I'm going to speak what's in my heart and on my mind—whether you want to hear it or not."

He threaded his fingers through her hair then cupped her cheek in his hand. "I enjoyed making love with you just now. Actually…" He paused to sit on the edge of the bed and pull her onto his lap. "Not enjoyed. Loved. You have no idea how amazing it felt to have you beneath me and me inside you as deep as I could go."

Able to feel the strength and heat of his arousal, she stared at him in disbelief. "Holden!"

Arms laced around her waist, he regarded her steadily. "And whether you want to admit it or not, you enjoyed it, too."

His honesty triggered something deep inside her, something she'd never dared face before. She tried to act with a coolness she couldn't really feel. "You want the truth?" she countered, unsure whether to kiss him again or send him away. "I loved making love with you, too."

His mesmerizing eyes met and held hers again. "So?"

Aware they were headed into dangerous territory, Libby said, "The fact that our chemistry is so good scares me."

"Why?" Holden countered calmly. "You know I'd never hurt you."

That was the problem. She looked down at her jeans and pleated the denim between her fingers. "I know you wouldn't mean to, any more than I'd mean to hurt you. But…" Her voice caught for a moment before she could go on. "Sometimes things that happen in the heat of the moment don't last."

Looking as conflicted as she felt, he ran his palms over her shoulders and down her arms, eliciting sensations everywhere he touched. "Are we talking about you and me now? Or you and Percy?"

Libby slid off his lap and sat beside him. "Percy." She sighed.

Holden took her hand gently. "I'm listening."

She grimaced. "I feel disloyal saying it."

He squeezed her hand before releasing it. Tenderly, he touched her face again, cupping her chin with his palm. "You owe yourself more than you owe him. You always have."

Her emotions in turmoil, Libby vaulted off the bed once again. "I know that. But it doesn't make it any easier."

Holden followed her to the window, where she stared out at the bleak darkness of the night. She knew she had to unburden herself to someone if she was ever to have any peace. She wanted it to be Holden.

She looked at him and forced herself to admit the truth. "Percy married me only because his parents wanted him to get married."

Holden did a double take. "What?"

An unsettling silence fell between them. "It came out in that last fight we had, before Percy went off to South America with you."

Holden's mood shifted from concerned to perplexed. "I don't understand."

"I told you that we were arguing about having a baby. I wanted one…he wasn't ready. In the heat of the moment he finally admitted that. If it hadn't been for unrelenting pressure from his parents to produce an heir that would one day carry on the family business, he said he never would have asked me to marry him."

Holden's jaw hardened. "That's true," he confirmed, beginning to see the full picture. "Percy's folks were on his case, big-time, right before he met you. They wanted a grandchild while they were still there to enjoy one."

She nodded, beginning to feel a little better now that this was all coming out. "And Percy thought I was perfect," she recalled with weary resignation, reciting the facts that had come out in her last awful argument with her husband. "I was shy and sheltered enough to please his parents and be easily malleable, with no familial commitments of my own to mess with his. And yet eager enough for excitement and adventure to do most anything he wanted, too."

"Sounds…calculated."

"I know." Libby hitched in a breath, forcing herself

to be fair. "But I don't think it was at the time. I believe Percy was just trying to please everyone while still being able to please himself. I think he thought it would work out. That our love for each other would be strong enough to withstand the dullness of everyday married life."

Holden leaned toward her. "Only it wasn't."

"Once the ring was on my finger," Libby admitted, "he lost interest in sex."

"That must have been devastating for you!"

Shrugging off the humiliation, Libby rushed on. "I told myself it was normal. That all couples went through that, and we couldn't stay in the honeymoon phase forever. And I concentrated on pleasing him in other ways."

Holden held her gaze. "But Percy didn't care about home-cooked meals or a nice apartment or your devotion to learning his family business."

"No." Libby smiled sadly. "He wanted adventure, in increasingly risky venues."

"Like rock climbing and white-water rafting and black diamond skiing."

She threw up her hands. "And I just couldn't do it. I was afraid. So—" she shrugged and moved away from the window "—I suggested he do more of those things with you, and he was happy for a time."

"Until?" Holden lounged against the wall while she paced.

"I told him I wanted a baby." Libby knitted her fingers together. "And then the sex pretty much stopped altogether."

She strode forward and forced herself to continue, despite the lump in her throat and the tears gathering behind her eyes. "I couldn't bear it if the same thing happened with you and me, now that we've gotten through the awkwardness that followed my hysterical pregnancy, and have started to become friends on our own."

"Which is why you need some space."

She warmed at the understanding in his level gaze. "Yes. I know you've been lonely, Holden. So have I. But I have to really think about this." She paused and drew an innervating breath. "Before we get into a place where we could do real damage."

"I COULD HAVE TOLD YOU agreeing to date Libby platonically was a bad idea," Kurt told Holden the next evening, when he went over to his cousin's house for dinner. "Setting up parameters like that boxes you in."

Paige handed Holden a cup of coffee and shooed everyone away from the dinner table. As she led the way to the family room, where the triplets were already playing, she stated her view. "Romances start all kinds of ways. Look at ours...." She flashed a grin at her husband, then turned back to Holden. "Kurt and I absolutely loathed each other—until the triplets were left on his parents' doorstep and I was drafted as their official foster mother."

"True." Kurt smiled, remembering his unconventional introduction to fatherhood. He sat down beside his wife on the sofa and kissed her temple. "Just goes to show what idiots we were."

Paige leaned over to kiss him back.

Holden held up a hand, only half teasing. "Guys! Stop with the PDAs." If he was going to work his dilemma out as quickly and efficiently as he wanted, he needed the two lovebirds' full attention. "I've got a problem here."

Paige straightened. Suddenly more love doctor than pediatric surgeon, she stated soberly, "Yes, you do. And it's more than the jelly and barbecue sauce that the triplets got all over your shirt during dinner."

Holden looked down at the mess, abruptly wishing he and Libby had such little domestic problems every day, instead of the really big one confronting them.

Kurt toasted him with a coffee mug. "If you want to pursue Libby, you have to forgot about your chances of success and go after her with everything you've got."

Paige snuggled into the curve of her husband's arm. "Kurt's right about that. We women respond to persistence."

That, Holden knew. It was the rest of the situation that bothered him. "How can we be sure it's not a rebound thing for either of us?"

Paige tightened her fingers on Kurt's forearm. "Is she still in love with Percy?"

Holden frowned. "I don't think so."

"Do you still have unrequited feelings for Heidi?"

"Definitely not."

Paige went to her computer and looked a few things up. Finally, she sat back in relief and said, "Then, technically, it can't be a rebound romance for either of you, no matter what you're calling it. For that to occur, you still have to be reeling from your breakup." She paused and looked up from the screen. "According to the experts, once you've come to terms with what happened, it doesn't matter how much time has or hasn't elapsed. It's safe to go on and start dating seriously again."

One problem down. "That's good to know," Holden murmured.

The big question was, how was he going to convince Libby that he would never lose interest in her the way her late husband had?

BE CAREFUL WHAT YOU WISH FOR, Aunt Ida had often cautioned. And in this situation, Libby thought Friday evening, her late aunt might just be right.

Libby had asked Holden to give her space.

And he had. For the past forty-two hours and thirteen minutes she had not heard from or seen the handsome rancher.

He hadn't even shown up for toddler library hours at her home. Miss Mim had served as her volunteer, helping patrons select and check out books. And now the two of them were headed to the Lone Star to meet Miss Rosa for dinner.

As Libby drove to the restaurant and dance hall, which was owned by Holden's mother, the retired librarian sized her up from the passenger seat. "You seem depressed, dear."

Libby was. So much so that she felt like crying. And she never cried.

"Are the holidays getting you down?"

"A little," she admitted.

The rest was Holden and the notion that she might be walking away from the best thing that had ever happened to her.

"The cure for the yuletide blues is staying busy."

Libby smiled. "I know. And I have been." She had even more activities planned for the upcoming weekend.

Sadly, none included Holden, who in just one week had become much more important to her than she could have imagined.

Miss Mim took her arm as they walked across the parking lot. "I hope you have your thinking cap on. Miss Rosa and I are going to need every bright idea you can muster up this evening."

"I'll do my best to be brilliant," she promised, tongue-in-cheek.

Miss Mim smiled.

Always happy to be helping someone, Libby smiled back.

Her spirits lifted even more as they walked into the restaurant. A beautiful tree stood in the lobby. Christmas music wafted from the stereo system. It being Friday evening, the place was crowded with families and couples on dates.

Greta McCabe met them at the hostess stand and showed them to a table by a window. "Your dinner partners should be here momentarily."

"Dinner partners?" Libby echoed in confusion. She thought they were only meeting Miss Rosa.

"I invited someone else to help us brainstorm ways to solve the library crisis," Miss Mim said, with sudden choir-girl innocence. "I hope you don't mind."

"Why should I..." Libby took in the librarian's sudden smile and followed the direction of her wave.

Holden McCabe. Of course.

Why had she not seen this coming?

And why did he have to look so devastatingly handsome in a black blazer, light blue shirt and well-fitting jeans?

"Ladies," Holden said, inundating Libby with his sexy scent as he neared. The familiar aromas of leather and soap mixed with the familiar masculine fragrance of his skin.

A shiver slid down Libby's spine as he paused to greet her with a casual hug and kiss to her brow that spoke volumes about his intentions—to everyone in the place.

Still smiling, he held out a chair for Miss Rosa, then paused to gallantly clasp Miss Mim's hand and say hello to her, too. Having worked his magic on all three women, he circled the table and sat down next to Libby, his knee nudging hers slightly as he settled his tall frame.

She looked into his blue eyes. And felt yet another whisper of desire.

"So," Holden said as soon as their drink and appetizer orders had been placed. He looked directly at Miss Mim, "I scouted around, just like you asked, and here's what I've been able to find out from the county commissioners."

"The news is bad, isn't it?" she fretted.

Holden nodded. He leaned back as tall glasses of mint-flavored iced tea were delivered, and baskets of fried onion rings and Southwestern egg rolls were put in the center of the table.

When the waitress had disappeared, he continued, "The estimate on the repairs needed to remove the asbestos and reopen the library has come in at close to a quarter of a million dollars."

Miss Rosa gasped. "That's more than our bare-bones operating budget for one year! It doesn't even include the purchase of new books or magazines."

"Let me guess," Libby said. "The county doesn't have the funds."

"And things are so tight right now there's no way to get them. So the plan they are going to present to the public, and vote on in January, is to keep the facility closed for one year, stockpile the unused operating funds and then start the repairs—which are estimated to take anywhere from three to six months—in December of next year."

"That's unacceptable!" Libby cried.

Holden gestured. "I told the commissioners the citizens weren't going to like it. They don't feel they have any choice."

"There's always a choice," Libby said, unable to contain her fury.

All eyes turned to her.

"Maybe the county doesn't have the funds, but that doesn't mean we have to sit back and take it," she fumed.

"We could try and raise the funds privately," Miss Mim offered.

Miss Rosa sighed. "But that would take a long time, too."

"And that's the other bad part," Holden said, looking at the young woman, who was just out of college. "They may have to let the entire staff of paid employees go, too."

"So I could be looking for a job." Miss Rosa burst into tears.

"Don't you worry about that," Libby said fiercely.

Holden nodded. "We'll all work together to find you something here in Laramie, with equitable pay, until the library does reopen. And the same goes for all the hourly employees. How many are there?"

"Three." Miss Rosa relaxed in relief.

Silence fell.

"Maybe we could approach some of the various charitable foundations in Texas to help us," Libby said. "We could start a letter-writing campaign, tell them what the community has already been willing to do to keep our library going. Who knows? Five thousand here, another two or ten there—if we can get enough help from all sorts of sources, we might just reach our goal."

Miss Mim smiled. "That's the spirit! I knew we could count on you. You always know what to do. There's no one better to lead a crusade."

And, Libby thought, if she sold her business as planned, she would definitely have the time to take it on.

The rest of the meal was spent brainstorming various ways to start the fundraising process immediately. By the time Miss Mim was ready to be driven back to her apartment in the Laramie Gardens Senior Center, they had a game plan to execute.

Libby started to rise.

Miss Rosa lifted a staying hand. "I'll drive her home."

"Yes, dear," Miss Mim ordered, with a wink aimed Holden's way. "You two stay here and enjoy your coffee."

The two librarians left.

"I think Miss Mim is matchmaking," Libby said.

The corners of Holden's lips turned up. "I think you might just be right," he drawled.

"I also think you might have something to do with it."

He chuckled. "I think you're right about that, too. Although, I did want to be here tonight for the library's sake, too. It's an important institution. It means a lot to the people of Laramie." His expression turned tender as he covered her hand with his. "The way you handled that crisis was quite impressive."

Libby blushed. She didn't know why his admiration meant so much to her. It just did. Modestly, she replied, "I haven't really done anything yet." *Except maybe fall a little harder for you....*

She swallowed emotionally. "You were great, too, by the way."

"We make a good team," he said with a gleam in his eyes.

They were certainly beginning to, Libby thought wistfully.

"Let's celebrate." He tugged her by the hand, took her onto the dance floor and spun her around.

"Holden?"

"Hmm?" His hand tightened around her waist, and he pressed his cheek against hers.

Libby sighed and tried not to feel too comfy. It was, as she might have predicted, a losing battle. Using her elbows, she wedged a bit of space between them. "The band hasn't started yet."

He glanced up at the empty stage. "Oh, yeah." With a bemused look on his face, he let her go. "Wait here."

Libby had no doubt Holden knew how to turn on the music. His mother owned the restaurant and dance hall, and he—like the rest of his siblings—had grown up working here, whenever they weren't toiling on their dad's horse ranch.

Seconds later, dance music poured from the speakers.

Libby flushed as he rejoined her and took her in his arms. "Am I supposed to be getting a message from all this?" she asked.

"I sure hope so."

Her heart skipped another beat as Lady Antebellum sang, "All I want for Christmas is you."

Chapter Ten

"That was some romantic gesture," Libby remarked several fun-filled hours later. Way past midnight, the Laramie streets were quiet. A full moon shone overhead in the black velvet sky. Christmas wreaths decorated the light posts all along Laramie's historic Main Street. Every storefront and business was decorated to the hilt, adding to the festive air. But best thing of all, Libby thought, was being here with Holden.

Just the two of them.

He smiled down at her. "I'm glad you liked dancing with me."

Libby shivered as the cold winter breeze blew against them. "You didn't have to keep spinning me around for the last four hours." They had closed the place down, which was another first for her. Leaving only when the rest of the staff bailed, too.

Holden tucked her into the curve of his body. "You know us Texans." Lazily, he guided her toward the parking lot. "Do it up big or don't do it at all."

Libby laughed and ducked her head, resting her cheek against the solid warmth of his chest. "I'm beginning to get that sense of you," she murmured.

Finally, they reached her Range Rover, with his pickup

truck several rows over. Standing in the parking lot, Libby wished Holden would build on what they had started and kiss her passionately.

Instead, he stepped back, shoved his hands in the pockets of his leather bomber jacket and said, "What are your plans for tomorrow?"

Libby blinked. "Tomorrow?"

"Saturday. You know." He spoke clearly, enunciating every word. "Do you have to work?"

Brought swiftly back to reality, Libby sighed. "Unfortunately, I do. Jeff Johnston is coming by the dealership with his accountant and his lawyer to take a look at our books and get more information, so he can estimate the value of Lowell Ranch Equipment and formulate a formal offer."

Holden ran a palm beneath his jaw. "You could do that for him, you know, simply by putting a price tag on the business."

Libby rocked forward onto the toes of her suede boots. "I'd rather he take the lead."

Holden's lips quirked in amusement. "So you can counter."

She preened. "I have learned a thing or two since I started working there, many moons ago."

Holden sobered. "I guess you have."

Silence filled with longing followed. Still he didn't kiss her, didn't make a move. Doing her best to stifle her frustration, Libby continued, "And then I promised to work a booth at the Community Chapel bazaar."

Holden inclined his head. "The kissing booth?"

If only, Libby thought. She gave him a droll look. "You know they don't have kissing booths at the church. In fact,

I don't think they have them anywhere anymore. Too many germs."

He nodded, deadpan. "It is flu season."

Libby smiled. She didn't know what his deal was. All she *did* know was that she couldn't get enough of him—and she sensed that this malady was only going to get worse.

"Which reminds me," Holden continued, looking down the street at the now-closed pharmacy. "I need to get my shot."

Libby winced. "So do I. I haven't had time for that, either."

Holden quirked a brow. "Want to do that together?"

Libby scoffed, not sure whether he was joking or not. "Get our flu shots?" she echoed, more intrigued with the cowboy in front of her than ever.

"We could keep each other on track. Stop the procrastination!" he teased.

"I guess we could at that," Libby drawled.

Serious now, Holden said, "They offer them at the pharmacy, you know. We could go over after the bazaar. Say around six? I'll even let the pharmacist know we're coming."

He meant it! About protecting them both from illness and spending time with her. "You'll make reservations," she repeated.

"Like I said." He shrugged easily. "It will keep us focused."

They needed that. "All right," Libby said impulsively. "You're on."

Hand to her spine, he guided her toward her car. "And after that, we'll see."

Libby rummaged for her keys and hit the unlock button on the pad.

Heart racing, she slanted Holden a sideways glance. "See what?"

"Don't know." Mischief sharpened the attractive lines of his face. "But it's a magical time of year." He looked deep into her eyes and contented himself with a light, friendly peck on her head. "Anything can happen."

"I HEARD WHAT WENT ON at the Lone Star last night," Paige said the next day, when she met up with Libby at the community center where the bazaar was being held. She playfully elbowed her. "Dancing without music?"

Libby tied on her change apron. "I know it sounds lame. It was actually…romantic." Unable to help herself, she flushed self-consciously.

Paige moved in for a closer look. "You both have it bad, don't you?"

Libby started straightening the boxes of donated chocolate candy and fruit baskets. "What do you mean?"

Her friend shrugged and set up the cash box. "I've never known Holden to make a fool of himself over a woman. Even with Heidi he was somewhat restrained in his affections."

He hadn't been restrained at all when Libby and he had made love. On the other hand…

Figuring she could use some perspective from a friend who had the happily-ever-after thing down pat, Libby remarked, "He was restrained last night."

Paige glanced at her, curious.

"He walked me to the parking lot." Libby winced, recalling. "But not even a kiss good-night."

Paige chuckled. "Second rule of male courtship—leave 'em wanting more."

Or maybe, like Percy, he didn't want her at all….

Libby pushed the disturbing thought away.

"He's being respectful of you," Paige said.

Libby harrumphed, thinking of the beautiful night and full moon and perfect opportunity that had gone to waste. "I didn't want gallant last night," she muttered in frustration.

Paige drew her to a corner of their booth, well out of earshot of others setting up. "Is that what you said to him?" she whispered.

"Well, no," Libby admitted, wondering if she would ever be able to go after what she truly wanted.

Still studying her, Paige stated, "So in other words, Holden is sticking to the prescribed plan laid out by you."

I guess. "Speaking of which." Having figured out Holden's lack of action was her own fault, Libby pushed on with the rest of her confession. "He asked me to go with him tonight to get our flu shots."

Her friend blinked in surprise. "The couple that vaccinates together, stays together?" Her eyes twinkled. "It's good, though. He lined up the next date. That means he is serious."

Libby pushed a strand of hair behind her ear. She had hoped for romance, but now that she had it, she didn't know what to do. "I'm very confused."

"Don't be." Paige hugged her. "Just go with it. Let fate show you what will happen next."

FOUR HOURS LATER, the church bazaar was over and Libby headed to the pharmacy. Holden got out of his pickup just as she pulled up beside him in the parking lot.

Looking handsome as ever, with his dark hair ruffled from the winter wind, he shoved his hands in the pockets of his bomber jacket and gave her a teasing once-over as she joined him.

"You're not going to faint on me, are you?" he asked.

Libby rolled her eyes and resisted the urge to lean in close to the protective shield of his tall, strong body.

Still feeling a little peeved that he hadn't given her a proper good-night kiss the evening before—no matter what she had said days earlier—she shoved her own hands in the pockets of her sophisticated red down jacket. "No. Of course not." Unable to resist, she slanted a mocking glance his way. "Are *you* going to faint on *me?*"

Holden rubbed his palm contemplatively along the rugged line of his jaw and peered at her in concern. "Maybe we should have some smelling salts on us, just in case."

Libby couldn't tell whether he was joking or not. She did know he had worked just as hard at the booth he and Kurt had run, as she and Paige had at theirs.

She slowed her steps as they reached the entrance, delaying the moment they actually went inside. Burning with curiosity, she asked, "Why did Kurt slap you on the back like that when we were leaving?"

Holden turned toward her and tucked an errant strand of her hair behind her ear, the backs of his fingers caressing her cheek slightly in the process. Then he shrugged. "Why do men always slap each other on the back?" he asked, all innocence.

"I don't know." Libby rocked forward on her heels and propped her fists on her hips. "Encouragement?" she guessed.

Holden nodded. "Exactly."

Libby told herself the satisfied gleam in his eyes had nothing to do with the passionate way they'd made love to each other a few nights earlier. "Why do you need encouragement?" she pressed.

Holden grinned and leaned in closer still. Almost close enough for them to kiss. "Why do you think?"

This flirting was beginning to be fun. It was also showing her a whole new side to Holden McCabe.

Maybe he wasn't so guilt-ridden and far too responsible for his own good, after all.

Maybe she had been wrong to insist on a sexual time-out....

He opened the door to the pharmacy and ushered her inside. Ten minutes later, they had both filled out their forms, paid the fee and received their injections. Band-Aids on, they were free to go. "So now what?" Libby said as he helped her with her coat and slipped his on, too.

Holden's hand moved to the small of her back as they made their way toward the exit.

Unfortunately, the aisle they had randomly chosen was filled with contraceptives and sexual aids and lotions. Appearing oblivious to the products lined up to the left of them, Holden leaned in closer and murmured in her ear, "Well, if we were still rebound dating, I know what we'd do."

So did Libby, unfortunately. If she spent any time at all alone with him, she would undoubtedly end up in his bed, enjoying herself every bit as much as she had before. Consequences be damned!

Trying not to flush, she hurried on down the aisle toward the safety of the greeting cards stacked at the other end. Then, taking his hand, she hurried Holden out the door and across the lot to their vehicles.

Only when they had were safely out of earshot of everyone did she release her grip on him.

Their eyes met, and she felt a heady sensation deep inside her. "You're trying to get me to change my mind," she accused. *About everything.*

"I'm trying to get you to take us off Hold."

Here was her chance.

She could play it safe, the way she had been.

Be loyal to everything she had known in the past.

Or take a risk.

AS THE SECONDS TICKED BY, Holden wasn't sure what Libby was going to do. He could see she was as deeply conflicted as he, that she didn't want to risk their fast-growing friendship with a more intimate relationship that might or might not work out, for even the short run.

"On one condition," Libby said finally, beginning to smile. "It has to be something fun. And holidayish."

Holden's tension eased. Playtime was something he could handle. Especially with Libby.

Given where they were standing, it didn't take long for the next idea to hit. "How about some holiday greenery for the front grilles of our vehicles?" Decorating your ride was a fine Texas tradition. One, as far as Holden knew, that she had never participated in.

"You're serious."

Having picked a winner, he raised his shoulder. "We'll make it a contest."

She slapped her thigh. "Now you're talking!"

Enjoying the lively spark in her dark green eyes, he continued the challenge. "Whoever has the best-decorated wreath wins."

Her lips curved in a delicious smile. "The winner—?"

Remembering the silky feel of her skin, wishing he could forgo convention and kiss her again, Holden decided, "The winner gets the meal of his or her choice. The loser cooks said meal."

Libby propped her hands on her hips and challenged him with a tilt of her chin. "Can you cook?"

He waggled his eyebrows. "There's one way to find out."

Laughing and teasing each other good-naturedly, they headed for the Kiwanis lot. It was crowded with people selecting trees, garlands and wreaths.

Holden and Libby concentrated on the latter.

Soon after, the next debate began.

She shook her head disparagingly at the wreath he was looking at. "Having one that large is ridiculous."

But Holden liked it. It wasn't sissy—it was man-size. He chucked her playfully on the chin. "Haven't you heard? In Texas, everything that is bigger—is better."

Libby struggled not to laugh. "I don't think that's exactly how the saying goes." She pursed her lips thoughtfully. "That medium size would be perfect for my Range Rover."

"I don't have a problem with that, as long as I get the large one for my pickup."

"Then size can't matter in the final analysis," Libby bargained.

Holden's eyes lit up in a way that told her he had found another meaning for her words. "I'm sure it won't," he said smoothly.

Libby flushed. "You're not going to behave yourself at all this evening, are you?"

She made it damn hard not to think about making love. "Hey—" Holden angled a thumb at his chest "—I figure as long as we're spending time together, we may as well be ourselves."

HOLDEN HAD A POINT, Libby knew.

For reasons she chose not to examine too closely, she wanted to drop her guard, too. Even though she suspected where that would likely lead. "Then I'll take the Mama Bear size and you can take the Papa Bear size," she said.

Holden grinned and paid for the wreaths. From there, they drove to the arts-and-crafts store. On a Saturday evening so close to Christmas, it was crowded with shoppers eager to pick up what they needed to complete their own decorating.

Libby headed straight for the yuletide aisles. She filled her shopping basket with red velvet ribbon, pinecones, and silver and gold ornaments while Holden stood patiently by.

Finally she turned. "Aren't you going to get anything?" she asked in consternation.

He regarded her with the same indulgence doting men used for their wives. "I was waiting for you to finish."

Libby swallowed, pushing the idea of marriage away. "I've got what I need. So you better get a move on, cowboy."

Grinning, Holden headed off to the college-sports section. He picked up a University of Texas banner, miniature longhorn cattle mascots, and footballs and basketballs.

"That's not Christmassy," Libby said with a perplexed frown.

He laughed, soft and low. "It is to me." Then he leaned down to whisper in her ear, "Where's your school spirit? You're a UT grad, too."

Tingling with desire, Libby straightened. "Men!"

He regarded her with comically exaggerated exasperation. "Women!"

And they were on.

After Libby paid for their purchases—over Holden's protests—the two of them went back to his ranch and spread their purchases out on the family-room floor. Holden turned on a Chris Botti Christmas CD. As the sexy trumpet music filled the room, they began working in earnest, ribbing each other all the while.

An hour later, they took their creations out to the driveway. Using coated wire, they attached three points of the wreaths to the front grilles of their respective vehicles, then stood back to judge their handiwork.

As Libby admired his breathtaking creation, she had to admit Holden had done a stellar job.

He had passed on a bow, and instead threaded the evergreen wreath with burnt-orange and white ribbons, the university colors. The official Texas banner was wired to the center of the wreath. Miniature longhorn mascots, footballs and basketballs served as ornaments.

Hers was equally gorgeous, though. She had tied a fancy, red velvet bow to the top of her wreath and studded the evergreen boughs with pine cones, and gold and silver ornaments.

"Much as I'm loath to admit it, I think yours is better," Holden said finally.

Libby shook her head. "Yours is definitely more original."

They exchanged grins.

He held out his hand. "A tie, then?"

She fitted her palm against his. "Agreed."

Their fingers remained entwined. "So...who makes who dinner?" he asked eventually.

Who cared about eating, when her date for the evening looked so sexy?

Telling herself all good things come to those who wait, Libby reined in her skyrocketing desire and suggested cheerfully, "Suppose we do it together?"

A sensual smile lifted the corners of his mouth. He seemed as eager to spend time with her as she was with him. "Good idea. Although I have to tell you, my fridge isn't nearly as well stocked as yours."

He wasn't kidding, Libby soon found out.

There was part of a chocolate-peppermint pie from his sister's restaurant. A gallon of milk, another of orange juice, a six-pack of Bohemia beer. A package of hot dogs and buns, mustard, ketchup and pickles. The pantry held a bag of chips.

"Looks like we're having an indoor cookout," she sighed.

"Sounds good to me."

As Holden built a fire in the fireplace, Libby located the long-handled forks for grilling. They set up picnic-style in front of the hearth. When he smiled at her, she suddenly realized that nothing was as simple as it seemed.

MOST WOMEN WOULD HAVE turned up their nose at the meager offerings in his fridge and insisted he take them out for a proper Saturday-evening dinner. It was only eight-thirty. There were plenty of places in Laramie still open.

But Libby seemed content to rough it right along with him. He was content just sitting there in the soft light, listening to the music and watching her.

"You keep smiling," he said after a while, aware that there was magic in the air and it was all due to her.

"I was just thinking about how happy I am right now."

Her lips curved in a gentle smile. "I haven't felt this much Christmas spirit in a long time."

Holden fitted a hot dog on a long-handled fork and gave it to her. "What were your holidays like as a kid?"

She shifted closer to the fire and held the meat over the burning oak. "Memories of the holidays with my parents are a little fuzzy, since they died when I was in elementary school, but I can remember them taking me to see Santa Claus at the mall, decorating a tree, having Christmas dinner in a restaurant."

There was such warm affection in her voice. "And after that—with your aunt Ida?" Holden prodded.

Libby moved over slightly, so he could cook his hot dog, too. "Aunt Ida was all about the little things," she reflected fondly. "Perfectly decorating the tree and the rest of the house, baking gifts for all the neighbors, caroling…. After she passed, the holidays lost a lot of its joy for me. But maybe that's because I let it…"

Holden's shoulder nudged hers as they both tried to keep their hot dogs from getting too close to the flames. "I remember Christmas with Percy's family was always a little tense."

"And for good reason." She handed Holden her fork and then set about opening up two whole-wheat buns. "All his parents ever wanted was to spend time with him. And all Percy ever wanted was to head for the slopes." Libby squirted on mustard. "He loved his folks, but he still had one foot out the door all of Christmas Eve, much to their displeasure. We usually left for New Mexico or Colorado right after present opening on Christmas Day."

Holden helped transfer the deliciously charred hot dogs to the buns. "And once you were there?"

She added potato chips to both their plates. "He skied

every second he could on the black diamond runs, which were way too difficult for me. So—" she sighed wearily, munching on a dill pickle "—we usually spent a lot of time apart. Although we'd usually meet up for a late dinner in a restaurant."

Holden opened a beer for her. "Did you ever try to change that?"

"You know Percy." Libby took a sip of the golden liquid. "He wanted what he wanted, when he wanted it...and that was that."

And, Holden was willing to bet, she had never complained.

He had loved his late friend, but in this respect, Percy had been a donkey's rear end, because Libby had deserved so much better.

"What about you?" she asked as they began to eat. "What were your Christmases like as a kid?"

Holden watched the play of firelight on her honeyed hair. "Just what you would expect." He shrugged. "Fun, loving. All the traditional stuff. Lots of family." He sobered. "That changed when Heidi and I got involved."

Libby finished her hot dog and munched on a chip. "How so?"

"The first December Heidi and I were together, we were just beginning our relationship. Heidi learned she was pregnant. The crisis colored the holiday."

"She wasn't happy?"

"Not really. Not the way I was." Again, Holden's shoulder touched Libby's as they turned their attention to the flames. "Looking back now, I realize she wasn't over her ex. At the time it happened, I thought it had to do with the fact that she was expecting a baby and we weren't married." Wearily, Holden continued, "Heidi knew her family wasn't going to like that—or the fact we had been dating only a couple of months. So we went to Cabo, to elope."

"And then in March, she miscarried," Libby recalled.

Holden nodded, the memory making him grim. The six months he had been married had been the unhappiest of his life, yet he'd felt like an utter failure when it all fell apart.

He swallowed and pushed on. "In June, Heidi told me she didn't love me, was never going to love me, asked for a divorce and left town."

A compassionate silence stretched between them. Libby reached over and took his hand and Holden exhaled. "Our marriage ended in September."

She looked down at their laced fingers. "And then you and Percy went off on that last trip, and he died later that month."

Holden gave her hand a squeeze, let go. "I haven't felt a lot like celebrating the holidays since."

Another silence fell, this one not so easy to bridge. "I understand," Libby said softly at last. "I used to feel the same way."

Holden noticed her use of the past tense. "And now?" he pressed, suddenly realizing how much was hinging on her answer.

For the first time in a long while, Libby looked at peace. "I'm thinking it's time to turn the page, start over," she said emphatically. "Really enjoy the holidays for a change."

Absorbing the sight of her, so lovely and intent, Holden grinned. Together, they stood and carried their dishes into the kitchen. "That being the case, maybe we should do something about that." He took her arm and led her back toward the living room.

"Like what?" Libby asked, her eyes sparkling as they settled back on the floor before the fire.

Desire welled inside him. "Like this."

Chapter Eleven

The next thing Libby knew, Holden's arms were around her and his head was lowering to hers. She gasped as their lips forged. Waves of anticipation swept through her and then his mouth was locked on hers in a slow, sexy kiss that stole her breath. She melted against him, her breasts pressed against the hardness of his chest.

He was so warm and so strong. So unbelievably tender in his pursuit of her. She felt completely overwhelmed by the exciting masculine taste of his mouth, the tantalizing stroking of his tongue and the sweet, evocative pressure of his lips. She sighed in contentment as he deepened the kiss even more, commanding and seducing. She felt the sandpapery rub of his beard, inhaled the unique leather-and-soap fragrance that was him and sank ever deeper into his embrace.

Still kissing, they shifted. He guided her backward, so she was lying on the rug before the fire. He was beside her, his leg wedged between hers.

Libby loved how he challenged her to stop trying to please everyone else, and worry instead about pleasing herself. She loved the reckless, womanly way he made her feel.

He wasn't afraid to take desire to the limit, and for the first time, he made her want to do the same.

It didn't matter if they loved each other, although she was beginning to feel as if she might be falling for him in a major way. It didn't matter if this was meant to work out for the foreseeable future, or just the holiday season. Libby wanted Holden. She wanted to feel alive. Blessed. And joyful. She wanted this gift of time and caring and passion. The intimate emotional connection only he offered. And this one holiday, she was going for it all.

HOLDEN HADN'T MEANT TO kiss Libby this evening.

Oh, he had known he would hold her in his arms again. He had known from the way she looked at him, whenever she thought he didn't see, that she felt the new yearning between them, too.

He *hadn't* planned to let his passion for her get ahead of him, or risk having her feel that this was something that translated only into physical needs.

He lifted his head. "I want to take it slow."

Libby flashed a sultry smile and kissed him again, seeming as enthralled by the free-flowing desire between them. "So do I."

Tenderness surged through him. He wanted to honor and cherish her in a way she truly deserved. And that meant taking his sweet time pursuing her. He wanted to give her all the consideration and latitude that she had so obviously been missing. "You know what I mean."

She looked up at him with misty eyes, making no move to pull away. "I know what would be wise, and I know what I want," she murmured, her heart pounding in cadence to his. "And they aren't the same things at all."

She kissed him once more, surrendering even as she was seducing.

Gathering her close again, he gave in to the feelings surging inside him. He kissed her long and hard, slow and deep, reveling in their burgeoning passion. Until he felt her trembling and drew back once again, wanting to make sure. "Libby…"

She arched against him. "Make love to me, Holden. Right now and right here. And I'll make love to you…."

The steadiness in her voice and eyes was all the invitation he needed. He swept off her sweater, her bra, her jeans. With her help, he dispensed with his shirt. Bare-chested, he stroked his hand down her body, charting the dips and curves. And still they kissed, the connection getting hotter and more erotic. Libby was wild in a way he could never have imagined, free and sexy and celebrating what they felt.

She made a muted whimper of pleasure when he captured her breasts. Luxuriating in the silky texture, he palmed the softness of the feminine globes and rubbed the erect tips with his thumbs, caressed them with his lips and tongue.

Determined this night would be every bit as memorable as he could make it, he moved back to her mouth, putting everything he had into the kiss. Her lips were pliant beneath his, giving and testing, her body soft and surrendering.

Aware that nothing had ever seemed as right as this, he set about exploring the rest of her. Removed her panties. Slid a throw pillow beneath her head, and stretched out beside her on the rug, knowing that every moment they delayed, their mutual gratification would be multiplied tenfold.

Libby locked eyes with him and reached for his fly. "I want you naked, too."

Not about to let himself get ahead of her, he chuckled. "In due time."

With a mixture of tenderness and primal possessiveness filling his soul, he kissed his way from the nape of her neck, across her breasts, to her navel.

The need he wanted to see glimmered in her eyes.

Feeling a little like a conqueror who had just captured the fair maiden of his dreams, he moved lower still. She gasped as he found the silkiest, sweetest part of her, the softness of her body giving new heat to his. Loving the fierceness of her response to him, he kept right on tantalizing her, until at last she fell apart in his arms. Satisfaction rushed through him, along with raw, aching need.

He moved upward, rubbing his chest against her bare breasts, savoring the feel of her budding nipples, then took her mouth in a slow, hot mating dance.

Libby moaned and shuddered once again. "Holden..." The sound was part praise, part plea.

Her palms slid around his back, massaging the muscles on either side of his spine, then dropping to the waistband of his jeans.

"Naked," she repeated insistently.

He grinned as she rolled him onto his back, moved over him and divested him of his jeans and briefs.

He caught his breath as she straddled his hips and moved slowly, provocatively lower. Found him with her hands and lips, kissing and caressing him in all the ways he had fantasized her doing. With her hair falling across his abdomen, she enticed him further, whispered playfully, "See? This is nice, too."

"Really nice," Holden agreed.

And then there was no more waiting. For either of them.

Not about to climax without her, and needing to possess her, he pulled her upward. He shifted her onto her back and stretched out over her, taking control once again.

"We can try something else later. Right now, I want you this way."

Her head fell back in an age-old gesture of feminine surrender that heightened the excitement between them even more. "I want you this way, too." Murmuring in pleasure, she wrapped her arms and legs around him and lifted her hips to his.

"I'm glad we agree." He penetrated her slowly, sliding his palms beneath her, lifting her and filling her as she opened herself up to him even more.

And then they were one, kissing each other hotly, moving urgently, coming together again and again until there was only this moment in time. This heat. This passion. This connection that neither one of them had expected to find.

Thrills swept through them, again and again, until there was nothing but this gift as they writhed together. Until there was no more denying their ardent yearning for each other, no more delaying the inevitable. Spirits soaring, they succumbed to the swirling pleasure.

And Holden knew what he hadn't before. He no longer saw Libby as his rebound romance, but as the woman he wanted—the only woman for him.

"COME WITH ME," Holden urged early the following morning, as Libby gathered up her belongings and prepared to head back to her house.

"I already told you I was planning to attend. Your mother sent me an email invitation for the brunch." It was going to be held at Shane and Greta's ranch. The only people who were attending, aside from herself, was their immediate family.

She hadn't been slated to go as Holden's date, Libby thought as she sat down to pull on her boots. More like an "informally adopted" member of the family. This was part of her and Greta's strategy to take some of the responsibility of looking after her from Holden's shoulders.

And had Libby not followed her own swiftly building desires and made hot, passionate love with Holden, the strategy might have worked.

Regret that she hadn't exactly done everything she could to make sure Holden was relieved of his feelings of guilt and responsibility toward her filled Libby's heart.

She was being selfish again. Reaching out to him, letting him be her lifeline and a way out of her own residual grief and loneliness. When what she should have been doing was helping him extricate himself from the promise he had made to her late husband.

Holden held out his hand to assist her to her feet. "I want us to go together."

Together, they headed down the stairs to the foyer. "And make a statement," Libby guessed, not sure how she felt about that. On one hand, she was as thrilled by the possessive note in Holden's low, sexy voice as she had been by the way he'd made love to her.

On the other…she had become involved with Percy far too swiftly, and look how that had turned out in the end. Holden had done the same thing with Heidi. Again, with disastrous results.

When it came to relationships, going slow seemed to be necessary for success. What she and Holden had done the night before—passionately making love and then falling asleep wrapped in each other's arms—was anything *but* cautious.

Undeterred, Holden helped her into her coat. "I want everyone to know we're dating."

Libby adjusted her scarf around her neck. "They already know that."

He lounged against the banister as she searched for her keys. "They knew we were on…and then off."

"And now we're on again." Flushing at her presumptuousness, Libby abruptly stopped talking. The last thing she wanted to do was take too much for granted here and end up being a burden to him in much the same way she had been to Percy. Belatedly, she looked at Holden in apology and amended, "Through the holidays, anyway."

The inscrutable look was back on his face. "How about as long as this works for both of us?" he suggested amiably, after a moment. "No need to put a time limit on it."

As he sauntered closer, Libby struggled not to notice how sexy and self-assured he looked.

He took her in his arms. "And, instead, let's take it one day at a time."

Which would give him an out, should he want one, she supposed. It was sort of a guarantee she wouldn't become a burden, once the initial excitement of their sexual coupling passed, and she was more than okay with that.

Telling herself she was doing this as much for herself, as for him, Libby murmured, "Okay."

"Don't you look pretty today," Greta told Libby two hours later, when she and Holden arrived at the Circle M for brunch.

Libby hugged Holden's mother warmly. "Thank you." She felt as if she was glowing, inside and out. And not just from the lovemaking. It was the sense of family she suddenly had, too. The knowledge she no longer had to be alone.

"Holden, you look happy, too."

He winked. "I am happy, Mom."

"I can see that," Greta said thoughtfully, giving her son a meaningful look.

Seconds later, they were surrounded by the rest of the clan. Hugs and hellos followed.

Holden went off for a word with his dad, ostensibly to help him empty ice into big, stainless-steel tubs, but it was clear more was going on than that.

Emily frowned at the tense exchange, visible through the kitchen window. "What's going on between Dad and Holden?"

Jeb's wife, Cady, shrugged. "No clue."

Hank's wife, Ally, kept a poker face. "I'm not sure, either," she said eventually.

Maybe not, Libby thought, studying Greta's careful, polite expression. But Holden's mother knew something.

Even if she wasn't about to reveal what, in front of Libby.

Just that quickly, the warmth Libby had felt when she'd joined the family gathering faded.

She'd had a glimpse what it would be like to be a McCabe. But she was a far cry from ever really being part of the clan. No matter how hard Holden's mother was trying to bring her into the fold.

"What happened?" Holden asked later, after the gathering had broken up and they were driving back to her house.

Libby turned to him. "Maybe you should tell me."

HOLDEN HAD KNOWN it was a bad time to talk, but his dad hadn't wanted to put it off. Holden turned his glance away from the wheel of his pickup long enough to ask, "You saw me outside with my dad?"

Libby folded her arms in front of her. The action served to emphasize the lush curves of her breasts beneath her open coat and Christmassy sweater. "All the women did."

That didn't necessarily mean anything.

Pink color sweeping into her cheeks, Libby continued her inquisition. "Was your father warning you not to get involved with me?"

"Is that what you thought?" Holden asked in surprise.

Her lips set in a feisty pout, she tossed her head. Strands of silky hair, already tousled from the wind, swished about her shoulders. "It would make sense."

"No, it wouldn't," he told her frankly, glad they were nearly at their destination so he'd be able to stop driving and focus all his attention on her. "My dad likes you. He wants to see me married again, and so does my mom."

Arms still folded militantly, Libby settled deeper into the bench seat. "Then…?"

Struggling to contain his own emotions, Holden turned on his left signal light. "I asked him—and my uncles—to do me a favor." Obviously, not a good move on his part. Holden slowed his truck as they reached the town limits. He grimaced, bracing himself for the fireworks ahead. "I'm not sure you're going to like it."

She released an indignant breath, looking so pretty that all he could think about was kissing her again. "Tell me anyway," she demanded.

He stopped at a traffic light. "I asked them to talk to everyone they knew in the business community throughout the state and find out what they could about Jeff Johnston."

Libby shifted toward him, clearly interested, her eyes narrowed in cool speculation. "And?"

"He's clean, as far as his dealings go. Everything in his process is legal and aboveboard."

Intimacy simmered between them. "I could have told you that. I had the dealership attorney, Claire McCabe, do a background check on Johnston before I ever even entertained the idea of selling to him."

Holden knew they were headed into dangerous territory. "There can be things about a person that don't show up in a background check."

Her brow furrowed. "Such as?"

"He's known to be a very tough negotiator."

Libby tilted her head and gazed over at Holden. "That hasn't been my experience. In fact, to date he's been more than willing to work with me, even agreeing to keep the Lowell name on the business."

The change in traffic light forced Holden to move on. "Don't you think that's odd?" He waved at a friend manning the Salvation Army holiday donation bucket in the corner.

Libby waved, too, then turned to scowl at Holden. "Jeff realizes the Lowell name is synonymous with quality. He knows full well that customers are going to be wary enough about the change, without altering the name and logo, too."

Holden couldn't argue.

"And," Libby continued heatedly, "this is a way to keep the memory of Percy and his ancestors alive in the hearts and minds of all the people they served over the years."

Holden turned again and headed toward the dealership. "I can't see that sentiment meaning much to a tycoon in the making like Jeff Johnston."

"It may not, but it means something to the employees who work at Lowell Ranch Equipment, and Jeff realizes what an integral part they all play in the success of the dealership. Our customers depend on the relationships they have built with our sales and service staff members."

Holden did not deny the personal touch went a long way. But there was also ego involved. He approached the driveway to Libby's home and turned into it, pulled up close to the house and cut the engine. "According to my dad, Johnston has put his moniker on everything he owns."

"Well, not in this case. Besides," Libby said, "with the plans Jeff has to build up the business by adding an internet component, he'll probably make much more than I do now. As will all the employees, since they're going to own five percent of the business, once the deal is set."

Holden only wished negotiating a deal of that complexity was easy. "So you're not in the least bit worried…"

"You don't have to worry," Libby declared. "I've got this handled."

Easier said than done, Holden thought, as he and Libby gazed at each other with mounting emotion. Especially given the promise he had made to Percy, and Holden's own private need to shield her from harm.

But that was a story for another day. Right now, he needed to keep them spending time together. And there was only one way to do that.

Chapter Twelve

Libby stared at Holden as if she couldn't possibly have heard him correctly. "His and her Christmas trees?" she repeated.

Holden knew he was pushing it, but if Libby really was going to leave Laramie and relocate elsewhere after the sale of her business and home, his time to woo her was limited. Too limited. He gestured expansively. "We already have his and her wreaths."

She angled her head, clearly unconvinced. A wealth of consideration came and went in her bemused expression. "I know you mentioned getting one from your ranch earlier, but given the time crunch…what's wrong with getting them from the Kiwanis lot?" she challenged softly.

He leaned closer, inhaling her seductive cinnamon perfume. She was dodging intimacy again. "Where is the fun in that?"

Without warning, the sparkle was back in her green eyes. She planted a gloved hand in the center of his chest, successfully holding him at bay. "I suppose," she said drily, "you're going to tell me?"

Holden wished he could do a lot more than that. But knowing he was going to have to be a lot more patient if he wanted to make her his, he said, "For maximum holiday enjoyment, we need to obtain our trees the old-fashioned way. Unless—" he paused and peered at her through narrowed eyes "—you're not up to the task?"

Libby glared at him. "Excuse me?"

"Well," Holden drawled, enjoying matching words and wits with her, "it could be a little arduous." He puffed out his chest and flexed his muscles, then made a show of studying her much more feminine and slender form. "Trekking through the fields to the woods." He made another show of studying her legs. "Locating the perfect trees for each of us. Chopping them down, dragging them back. Yeah." Holden let his gaze drift slowly over her midriff before returning with taunting deliberation to her face. "You're right. Such rigorous physical activity on such a beautiful winter afternoon probably is a little much to expect you to do."

"Please." Libby rolled her eyes and released her seat belt. "I am certainly up to the task. All I need is a proper pair of boots and warmer clothing."

Because she said she would be "just one sec," Holden waited in the truck while she dashed inside. Five minutes later, she came rushing back out again.

Gone were the dressy sweater and slacks she had worn to brunch. In their place were a nicely worn pair of midnight-wash jeans, cream-colored thermal underwear beneath a trendy red-and-black buffalo-plaid flannel shirt and a vest with a marled sheepskin lining. She had tucked a flat-brimmed, dark brown Stetson on her hair and put rugged, shearling-lined boots on her feet.

She looked incredibly sexy—all fine Texas woman— striding toward him. Holden felt his heart thump in his chest.

Damn, but she was beautiful.

And until now, so underappreciated.

He promised himself she would never feel like a "ball and chain" to anyone again.

LIBBY HADN'T EXPECTED TO have such fun, driving and hiking all over Holden's ranch. But as they climbed fences, navigated rocks and traversed the rugged terrain where he taught and trained his cutting horses, she found herself laughing more and more.

"I think you know where the best trees are," Libby teased, enjoying the brisk winter weather as much as the rugged rancher leading her on this merry chase. "You're just pretending you don't."

Holden flashed her a sexy grin, denying nothing, then turned his attention back to the grove of mostly mesquite and a few gnarled live oak trees. With nary an Afghan pine in sight.

Abruptly all victorious male, he reached up and grabbed a bushy growth from an oak. He snapped it off, then showed the familiar green leaves and white berries to her. "Maybe this is what I've been looking for."

Libby stroked the plant reverently. "Mistletoe!" she said in surprise, her mind automatically shifting to thoughts of kissing Holden beneath the symbolic evergreen leaves. Now, that was romantic!

"Yep." He broke the mass of greenery in half. "One for you. And one for me."

She looked at the cluster. "His and her mistletoe?" Libby held up her portion, deciding it could be cut up even more, into manageable little clumps. Maybe tied with red ribbon…

"This way we'll both have some handy whenever the need arises," Holden told her with a wicked smile.

Her pulse racing almost as much as her fantasies, Libby threw back her head and laughed. "You are something, Holden McCabe!"

He grinned and held out a hand, to help her climb back over the fence they had just vaulted.

"Now we'll go look for the trees," he promised, wrapping a proprietary arm about her waist.

Ten minutes later, he had driven his pickup to a small grove of what looked to be cultivated pine trees along the edge of his property.

Libby braced her hands on her hips, studied the selection and shook her head. "You knew these were here all along."

Holden acknowledged it to be true, with a slight shrug and an insufferable wink. "Yeah. I just didn't know where the mistletoe was."

She rolled her eyes at his bad-boy antics. This was a side of him she didn't see enough.

He got the ax out of the truck, then stood back, admiring the small grove. "So which one do you think you want?" he asked.

Enjoying the fragrance of pine and the wintry sunshine, Libby studied a six-foot-tall tree with well-spaced branches. She walked back and forth, observing it from all angles and taking her time. Finally, she sighed. "That one, I think."

Holden's blue eyes were twinkling as he gazed down at her. "Sure you don't want a taller one?"

He was obviously going to draw this out as much as possible, insuring they spent more time together. Libby didn't mind at all. Playing the flirt to the hilt, she plastered a breezy smile on her face. "I'll leave the eight-foot one to you."

"Suit yourself." Holden cut down one, then the other.

Together, they dragged them toward his pickup.

"Since we're already here, we'll put mine up first," he said.

Libby knew it was imperative to get the tree in water as soon as possible, to keep it fresh. She was standing close enough to see the quarter inch of beard on the underside of his jaw that he'd missed when he last shaved.

Inhaling the scent of man and soap, she asked, "You want to decorate it, too?"

"Can't." Holden put his tools in their case and shut the tailgate of the truck. Pressing his hand against her spine, he walked her around to the passenger side. "I don't have any more UT stuff to put on it." He took two bottles of her favorite sparkling water from his truck and handed one to her.

Pleased by his thoughtfulness, Libby uncapped her beverage and took a long drink. She studied him over the rim of the bottle. "You're really going to decorate your Christmas tree in burnt-orange and white?"

The mischief was back in his eyes. "It'll be unique," he claimed, toasting her silently. "And it will match the wreath on my pickup."

"Well—" Libby walked around to take another look at the Christmas wreath attached to the front grille of his pickup "—never underestimate the powers of coordinated decor."

Holden chuckled. He lounged against the truck and clapped a companionable hand on her shoulder. "What are you going to put on yours?"

Libby stalked off through the calf-high grass. In the distance, she could see some of Holden's incredibly beautiful quarter horses grazing contentedly in the pasture.

She could understand why he liked living on a ranch. It was so peaceful out here. So pretty and still so wild in places, too.

She whirled around and walked toward him, not stopping until they were toe-to-toe once again. "I'm not sure yet."

He peered at her curiously. "You don't have any decorations at the house?"

She sighed. "I do, but…Percy's mom was all about symmetry. Her trees had to have one color ribbon and one type of ornament, and that was it."

Holden winced. "I remember."

Libby reached out to pick off some pine needles that were stuck to the fleece lining of Holden's jacket. "She varied it from year to year, but…"

"Doesn't suit you?" he guessed.

Finished, Libby stepped back again. "I'm a very disciplined person, but not in that area."

"What about decorations you used growing up?" Holden cocked his head playfully. "Still have any of those?"

"Aunt Ida liked glittery ornaments. Unfortunately, they are all so old the exterior is constantly flaking off."

"Not good," he commiserated.

"Not at all." Libby looked in his eyes, surprised at the banked desire she found there. "So I've been thinking, while we were traipsing your entire property, Holden McCabe, that maybe it's time I got new decorations, too." She lifted a hand in warning. "Before you get too excited, no burnt-orange and white."

His eyes crinkled at the corners. "Traditional all the way, hmm?"

Not always, Libby thought, considering the rebound relationship she had agreed to have with him. "We'll see.

I think I want to look around first," she confided, more eager for a fresh start than ever. "I think I'd like to get something really special to start my own collection with."

"Sounds nice."

It did, Libby thought. But what was even better was the joy she felt being there with him.

IT WAS JUST STARTING TO get dark when Holden and Libby arrived at her place.

She hopped down from the cab before he'd even cut the motor. Her long legs eating up the drive, she circled around to the back. "You don't have to carry my tree in, Holden. You can just leave it on the front porch."

He knew she could manage the tree on her own. The question was, why did she want to?

Frowning, he hefted the pine onto the ground. "Is there some reason you don't want me to come inside?" Was she afraid he was going to put the moves on her?

Despite his own desire, he'd managed to control himself thus far....

"Well, now that you mention it—" she pulled her keys out of the pocket of her jeans "—the place is a little messy."

Holden shrugged, not sure where this sudden tension and evasiveness was coming from. "I'm a guy. Mess is my comfort zone."

Still Libby hesitated.

Had he done something? Said something? Holden thought worriedly. Everything had been fine up to now....

Finally, she shrugged and said, "You're going to find out, anyway."

Find out what? Holden wondered as she led the way inside.

He got the tree just past the threshold, when he stopped in shock.

The Lowell family photo gallery that had lined the stairs and the foyer had all been taken down. The frames were stacked on the dining-room table. Additional boxes littered the floor.

A hammer and a jar of nails sat midway up the stairs.

Libby laid her clump of "his and hers" mistletoe on the foyer table, took off her vest and hat, and hung them on the coat tree next to the door. Flushing, she gestured. "That's as far as I got yesterday morning before I had to leave for the Community Chapel bazaar."

Holden was glad the photos of Percy and his ancestors had come down. It was yet another sign that Libby was ready to move on.

"What made you decide to do this now?" he asked, carrying the tree on into the family room at the rear of the house, where she had said she wanted it.

"Several things, actually," she murmured, opening the door off the kitchen and going into the garage.

She returned with a Christmas tree stand.

"Jeff Johnston is sending over a bank appraiser and broker on Monday afternoon, to evaluate the property. The local broker I had here on Friday morning said if I was serious about selling and getting the best price possible, I should start stripping the home of personal memorabilia."

Libby put the stand where she wanted it.

Holden set the tree inside. "Is that the only reason?"

"No," Libby said quietly. "I've been meaning to do it for a while now, I just haven't been able to figure out what I should do with all the pictures."

While she held the tree, he knelt to tighten the screws that would hold it in place.

"Normally, in a situation like this, the thing to do would be to return the photos to Percy's remaining extended family," she murmured.

Holden saw her dilemma. "Only there aren't any."

Her shoulders slumped. "I thought about taking them over to the dealership, but many of them—like the ones of him catching a fish or climbing a mountain—are far too personal for that. Plus—" she exhaled, her inner turmoil evident "—they don't have anything at all to do with tractor sales. Any of the Lowell family archives that do are already at LRE."

Holden kept his eyes locked with hers. "You could distribute them to old family friends."

Libby sighed, looking even more vulnerable. "The question is, who would get what, and how would I go about it?"

No question, it wouldn't be easy. "Do you want me to help you with that?" Holden asked her gently.

She shook her head, withdrawing emotionally again. "That's something I should do, as Percy's widow. But there is one thing you could help me with, if you're so inclined?"

He straightened, his own feelings turbulent. "Whatever you need," he told her sincerely.

Libby flashed an appreciative smile. "Help me finish removing all the photos from the frames, and take the picture hangers out of the wall."

For the next hour and a half they worked side by side, pausing to look at the photos they removed. Eventually, after studying one particularly poignant shot of Percy and his folks at his college graduation, and another one of all four of them on her wedding day, Libby shook her head in consternation and murmured, "I know it was just ten years ago, but this seems like it was from another lifetime. One that's getting harder and harder to remember."

Holden knew what she meant. His own marriage seemed light-years ago, too.

Their circumstances were different, though. He had opted out; she hadn't. He covered her hand with his own. "Does that upset you?"

"It used to." Libby leaned into his touch. "Now what I feel is more like relief." She swallowed and turned to search his face. "Does that make me a bad person?"

"No, Libby, it makes you human. And ready to move on." He wrapped his arms around her and hugged her fiercely. "And those are both good things."

"You've been hard to get ahold of," Miss Rosa told Libby at nine the next morning.

Libby blushed. She had been really busy.

"Anything you want to tell us about?" Miss Mim winked.

"Actually, yes." Libby sidestepped the subject of Holden and the fact that they had recklessly spent at least part of the night together yet again—at his ranch, in his bed.

She still couldn't bring herself to ask him to stay the night in her house yet. There was still too much of Percy there.

Libby went to her desk and got two copies of the fund-raising letter she had drafted. "Read this…and tell me what you think."

"It's fantastic," Miss Rosa said, when she had finished.

Miss Mim enthused, "You did a great job explaining how much the institution means not just to Laramie, but all of Laramie County. We'll get it sent out right away."

"You're welcome to use the computer and printer here in my office," Libby said.

Miss Mim hesitated. "Are you sure we won't be in the

way? We compiled a list of one hundred charitable foundations in Texas we want to try. So it's going to take a while...."

"That's fine," Libby assured them with a smile. "I'm going to be at the house, anyway."

Libby left the librarians and headed toward the exit. As she walked past the break room, she overheard a group of male employees talking.

"What do you think our annual bonuses will be?" Manny Pierce was asking the dealership accountant.

"Depends, but at five percent of the current profits, you can each figure on taking a very nice vacation..."

Her nerves jangling, Libby kept going.

Her aunt Ida had always said it was very bad luck to count your chickens before they hatched.

Libby had found that to be true.

As she reached the exit, Jeff Johnston was pulling up in his Maserati. Four more vehicles turned in right behind him.

The two men and two women congregated alongside Jeff. He introduced his attorney, bank appraiser, chief financial advisor and real-estate broker.

Libby hadn't expected an entourage, but she refused to let it rattle her. Smiling, she said, "Let's get started, shall we?"

The tour of the dealership, inventory and warehouses commenced. Finished with that, they headed across the road to the Lowell home. And it was there that the trouble began.

Frowns abounded as they toured the premises. Although he had been there briefly before, with no complaints, it was pretty clear today that Jeff was not impressed with anything he saw.

He returned to the living room, where the toddler section of the Laramie Public Library was now set up. "This is going to have to go—immediately," he said. "And the same goes for the information and help desk set up in the corner of the dealership showroom."

"Neither of those things are going to happen until we find a solution for the library crisis," Libby retorted.

Concerned looks passed among Jeff's team.

He paused. "You know, for tax purposes I want to close on this deal before December 31."

Libby nodded. "That still gives us twenty-one days."

"That's not a lot of time," his attorney remarked.

Jeff continued looking at Libby. "Mrs. Lowell is right," he said carefully after a moment. "That's plenty of time for me to get everything I want."

HOURS LATER, Holden and Libby were roaming the stores in San Angelo's Sunset Mall, looking for decorations for her tree. While they shopped, they talked.

"So Johnston and his group made you uneasy today," Holden gathered, when Libby had finished relating the morning-long tour.

She left one shop and headed for another, Holden right beside her. "It wasn't anything he said or did precisely."

Holden slid his hand beneath her elbow and brought her in close to him. "Just a feeling."

Libby nodded and continued walking. Once again, his hand kept contact, this time pressed to the middle of her spine. "I think the info your dad scouted on Jeff might be right." She sucked in a breath. "He probably is going to play hardball with me. He just hasn't started yet."

Holden leaned down to whisper in her ear. "If you want

backup, I'm here. And so is any other McCabe you'd like to bring along."

As tempting as it was, Libby knew that relying too heavily on Holden would not be good. Using him as a sounding board was one thing; employing him as protection another. "Thanks. But I think your aunt Claire can handle this for me." It was, after all, what her attorney was paid to do.

"Say, what do you think of this angel?" Libby paused to admire a particularly beautiful tree-topper.

Holden studied the dazzling ornament. "I think she looks like you. Seriously. Honey-blond hair, gorgeous face, emerald eyes."

They were flirting again, Libby noted, and she was enjoying Holden's teasing more than ever. She wrinkled her nose playfully at him. "So does that mean you think I should get it?"

He shrugged, pretending to misunderstand the question. "Unless you plan to sit atop your tree as the lead decoration."

Libby chuckled at the ridiculousness of the idea. "I meant, should I get an angel or a star? Because these glittery gold and silver stars are awfully nice, too."

"I see what you mean." Holden rubbed his jaw as he studied them gravely.

"And...?" Libby moved close enough to inhale his special scent.

He stepped even nearer, the heat from his body engulfing her. "I have no clue. I'm not an expert on interior design."

"What are you an expert on?" she asked.

Holden paused. For a second, she thought he was going to say something romantic to her. Instead, he pointed to a display of college ornaments and said, picking up a box for himself, "All things Texas, of course."

Chiding herself for wanting this fling of theirs to be more than they had agreed upon, Libby moved farther down the aisle, past the Western-themed decorations, toward the next grouping. Without warning, she found herself standing in front of a display of baby's first ornaments. Next to that was a selection of porcelain bride and groom and wedding-bell decorations.

She stopped to briefly examine both, before she was swamped with such wistfulness she had to turn away or risk bursting into tears.

"It's going to happen," Holden told her. He shifted the box to his other hand and cupped her face with his palm, stroking her cheek tenderly with his thumb. "Maybe sooner than you think."

Libby only wished getting what she really wanted for Christmas—a husband and a baby and a completely new lease on life—was that easy.

Holden's gaze probed her slowly and deliberately. "You're going to get the baby you've wanted for so long," he said.

She gestured listlessly, feeling tears threaten once again. "Not without love and marriage and all the traditional things that go along with it." Why was she suddenly feeling so moody? Up one minute, down the next…!

"Including courtship." He gave her shoulder a reassuring squeeze.

"And a man who doesn't view me as an unwanted burden or responsibility."

"You'll get that, too," he promised softly.

Would she? Holden seemed so sure. Fighting off a new wave of emotion, Libby swallowed and moved on to yet another aisle of decorations, these more her current speed. "I think I know how I want to decorate my Christmas tree."

She pointed to the row of individual ornaments, of every theme and variety. "I'm going to make a completely asymmetrical, one-hundred-percent-whimsical tree. As a symbol of my moving on."

Holden smiled and caught her hand in his. "Sounds good to me."

Chapter Thirteen

"I'm surprised to see you here—alone—again," Emily remarked when Holden sought her out on Thursday evening. As usual during the holidays, his baby sis was working late. Hence, even though the Daybreak Café had officially closed after the lunch rush, Emily was back in the restaurant kitchen at eight that evening, making some of the dough and batter that would be baked and served the following day.

Usually, though, her husband hung out with her. Holden took a seat at the stainless-steel work counter. "Where's Dylan?"

Emily shaped dough into candy canes. "At our ranch, hosting a 4-H Club workshop on the best way to get a green horse used to the saddle. So what's up?" She paused to wipe her hands on her apron. "Are you just here to see if I will feed you dinner—as you know I will?" Her expression gentled. "Or is something else on your mind?"

"I've already eaten, thanks." Holden rested his forearms on the table. "I came to get some advice."

Emily lifted her eyebrows. "This is new."

"Go easy on me." He scowled. "I'm struggling here."

His sister poured him a cup of coffee and brought out

a platter of cookies for him to peruse. "Obviously, this is about Libby and your crazy rebound deal with her."

Holden selected a thumbprint cookie with a strawberry center. "We're past that." He munched on the delicious confection.

"Oh?" Emily started shaping Christmas coffee cakes.

Holden worked to contain his frustration. "We agreed it would just go however long it goes. Into the spring, or before the holidays end." Realizing their affair could be over even sooner than he'd thought caused him to worry. And Holden wasn't used to worrying about romance.

Emily slid the dough into the oven and paused to set the timer. "Is that why you and Libby haven't been buddying around together the last three nights?"

Was it that obvious he was getting the heave-ho? Deciding maybe he was overreacting, Holden stuck to the facts. "I saw her Monday evening. We went shopping in San Angelo to get ornaments for our trees."

Emily cut peanut-butter fudge into neat one-inch squares. "What about Tuesday?"

Holden helped himself to a frosted sugar cookie. "She had an appointment with the outside accounting firm auditing her business, in advance of the sale."

"Wednesday?"

"A meeting with her attorney."

Again his sister lifted an eyebrow. "Tonight?"

Holden tensed. "She said she's not feeling well."

Emily mulled that over. "And you're not buying it?" she guessed.

He shrugged. "It is flu season. We both had our shots last weekend, but the pharmacist said it takes two weeks for them to become fully effective."

"I haven't heard of anyone being sick here in Laramie

just yet, but that doesn't mean she didn't pick up something when you were in San Angelo the other night."

"So you don't think she's just making excuses to try and cool things off between us?"

His sister paused. "Is there some reason you think that might be the case?"

Holden wasn't sure. "Things have been moving pretty fast."

A knowing smile crossed her lips. "Too fast for her?" Emily asked pointedly. "Or too fast for you?"

"Too slow for me," Holden clarified. He threw up his hands in exasperation. "I'm not sure about her."

Emily patted him on the shoulder. "Well, then, brother dear, there is only one way to find out."

LIBBY WAS HALFWAY THROUGH changing the sheets and comforter on her bed when the doorbell rang.

She glanced at her watch. Nine o'clock? Who would be stopping by this late? And without calling first!

Swearing at the inconvenience, as well as her dishabille, Libby stepped over the pile of discarded linens and headed down the stairs. A glance through the peephole in the heavy wooden door gave her the answer she needed.

Feeling equally thrilled and dismayed, she opened the door. Using flirtatiousness as a shield, she propped one hand on her hip and approximated her best Southern belle voice. "Why, Holden McCabe, is that you beneath the red-and-white Santa hat?"

He grinned, then bowed to her like a courtier. "It is indeed."

Her glance drifted to the items in his hand. "What's with the wreath and the bag?"

"The wreath is for your front door, since you don't have one yet. You'll notice it's very traditional,"

Meaning, Libby thought, it didn't have any sports memorabilia or university colors on it. Instead it was adorned with red and white berries woven throughout, and a big, red velvet bow.

She smiled at his teasing and accepted the gift gratefully. Together, they used the hook provided to hang it on her front door. Libby centered it just so, then stepped back to admire it. "It's very nice, thank you." Shivering in her yoga clothes, she ushered him in.

"As for the other…" Holden stepped over the threshold, shut the door behind him and handed her the bag. "I brought you some chicken soup from the Daybreak Café."

Normally, that sounded great. Tonight it made her want to barf. Again. Just catching a faint whiff of it made her hold up her palm and back away. "Thanks, but…"

Holden shrugged out of his jacket, and tossed it and his Santa hat on the coat tree next to the front door. He peered at her closely, his expression concerned. "You really are ill, aren't you?"

Libby knew her skin was an odd grayish color again; she could feel it. Wishing her heart would stop racing and her knees cease trembling, she clapped a hand over her abdomen. Working to sound a great deal more matter-of-fact than she felt, she explained, "I've got tummy troubles. I'm not sure why. It may have something to do with the chicken-salad sandwich I had at lunch. It tasted odd, but I was so hungry I was weak-kneed, so I ate it anyway, and have been paying for it this evening."

"Bummer."

"No kidding. I made it only halfway through my yoga workout when I upchucked all over my mat. So…that's why I begged off seeing you tonight." She hadn't wanted to go into the gory details.

He walked with her to the family room. Saw the bags and boxes right where they had left them on Monday evening. "Still haven't decorated your tree?"

Libby sighed. "No time."

He leveled an assessing gaze on her and kept it there. "What can I do to help?"

Libby pulled in a stabilizing breath. "Honestly? Nothing. I was just changing the linens on my bed. I was going to take a shower and go to bed." *And hope I don't throw up again.*

He gave her a long look that spoke volumes. "I can help with that," he offered.

She swallowed around the parched feeling in her throat and made a joke to lighten the tension between them. "The shower?"

"The bed making," he replied in a humorous way that made her heart skip a beat.

Their glances met and held.

Wishing she felt well enough to spend the evening with him, Libby sighed.

He clapped a hand to her forehead and frowned. "No fever."

Without warning, she felt weak-kneed again. Dizzy and trembling all over.

The last time she had felt like this had been in the first months after Percy died.

Libby swore silently to herself and closed her eyes. She could not go through this again.

IT DIDN'T TAKE A MIND READER to know that Libby wasn't telling him everything, Holden thought, as he accompanied her upstairs and helped her finish changing the sheets on her bed. Clearly, she was worried about the way she was feeling. He studied her pale skin and slightly shaky demeanor. "You sure you're okay to get in the shower by yourself?"

She scoffed, "I wouldn't do it if I didn't think I could."

A mixture of gallantry and tenderness surged through him. He touched the side of her face, not sure when he had felt such overwhelming devotion or responsibility for another human being. "Okay." He decided her color had almost returned to normal. "But I'll be right outside the bathroom door. So if you need help," he told her sternly, "you just call me."

Libby picked up the nightclothes she had already laid out, and cradled them in her arms. She took a moment to scowl at him. "I think I'll survive."

Heaven help him, he wanted to make love to her, here and now.

She slipped inside the bathroom and shut the door behind her.

Holden heard the water start.

By the time she emerged, her hair wrapped in a towel, prim and proper flannel pajamas on, he had her bed turned down and all ready for her. Wishing he could climb under the covers with her, Holden kissed the top of her head. "In you go."

She huffed in exasperation as he drew the covers up and tucked them in around her. "You're really overdoing it, you know."

Finished, he rested a palm on either side of her. "I'm also spending the night," he confided gently. "On the family-room sofa downstairs."

"You don't have to do this," she protested weakly.

He caught her hand, brought it to his lips and kissed the back of it. Still holding her eyes, he whispered, "I want to. And I'm not taking no for an answer."

LIBBY WOKE TO SUNLIGHT streaming through the windows. It took her only a moment to realize that the nausea and dizziness she had felt the night before were gone.

The desire she felt for Holden, when she walked downstairs and found him puttering around her kitchen, increased by leaps and bounds.

He looked incredibly attractive with his shirttail hanging out, the morning beard lining his jaw, his dark hair rumpled.

Turning, he regarded her with tenderness. "How are you feeling?" His voice was a sexy rumble.

"Much better, thanks."

Surprised by the emotions sifting through her, Libby sat down at the kitchen table. If she had been attracted to Holden before, it was nothing compared to how she felt now, after experiencing his kindness and consideration.

This was what an intimate relationship should be like. Two people caring for and depending on each other. Putting the other person's needs ahead of their own.

Holden set a plate of toast, a cup of her favorite peach tea in front of her.

By the time they had finished eating breakfast together, Libby knew she was well enough to go to work, so he decided to head out to his ranch.

She walked him as far as the front door. Taking a page from the man's playbook, she decided to try and line up their next date. "Want to come back tonight? It's Friday. I'll fix you dinner. You can help me decorate the tree."

Holden's face fell. He gave her a look more potent than

any kiss. "I'd love to, but I already promised to deliver a couple quarter horses to a ranch outside Wimberly today. I won't be back until late." He smiled. "Rain check? For Sunday evening, maybe?"

Libby had missed seeing him this week on the days they had been apart. Missed having time to talk to each other. Missed making love even more. "Sunday evening sounds good." Even though she would have preferred it to be sooner.

Holden paused, looking as if he wanted to say something, but wasn't sure he should.

Following a hunch, Libby drawled, "You may as well come out with it. Otherwise, I'm going to be wondering all day long what's on your mind."

He exhaled. "You know the bowl games start tomorrow."

It took her a moment to follow what he was saying. "Football?"

He chuckled. "Yeah. Football."

Or in other words, the sport that was so popular it was almost considered a religion in Texas. It was all the guys at the dealership talked about when they weren't with customers. "I thought the Rose Bowl wasn't until January," Libby said.

"It's not."

"And UT is in that, right?"

Holden nodded. He came close enough that she could feel his body heat. "But the rest of the games are exciting, too. And my brothers and I have a tradition of placing bets with each other, and watching as many of the games as we can together."

"Sounds fun."

"It really is," he said with a grin.

Libby nodded. If there was one thing she had learned at an early age, it was how to be a good sport. "Then I wish you luck."

"Actually, I was hoping for more than that." He took her hand in his and clasped it warmly. "Tomorrow it's my turn to host the gathering at my ranch. There are three games—the first is at 1:00 p.m., the second at 4:30 and the third begins at 8:00 in the evening."

That was a lot of football, Libby thought. And though she'd never been all that interested in it, she was interested in Holden. "So you are going to be busy."

"Very. Given the fact that my brothers and sister and their spouses and kids, plus our parents, will all be there for the party. So I was wondering..." Holden tightened his grip on her hand and gave her a look that caused her heart to flutter.

"If you think you're up to so many televised sports and McCabes in one day...would you be my date?"

"THE KEY TO ENJOYING YOURSELF is to place bets on the games, too," Emily told Libby, as the two of them set out platters of wings and veggies, supplied by her café.

There was only one tiny problem with that, Libby thought. "I don't know anything about the teams that are playing."

Emily smiled mischievously. "Then do what I do, and bet against whoever your husband—or love interest—is backing."

Libby flushed self-consciously. Sex and friendship weren't the same thing as love. "Holden and I aren't exactly..."

Holden passed by with a tub of beers and soft drinks on ice. He paused to kiss the slope of her neck in a decidedly possessive way. "Yes. We are." He winked at them both and took off.

Emily's eyes gleamed with a speculative light. "Wow...I don't think I have ever seen my big brother that smitten."

Still tingling from the tender warmth of his caress, Libby looked in the direction the handsome rancher had gone. "We're just..." she sputtered.

"Falling in love."

Libby was so startled she practically dropped the blue-cheese dip. "No."

Emily chuckled. "Deny it all you want." She set out a fruit platter and yogurt dip, confidence radiating in her low tone. "I know what I see. And don't forget to sign up for your teams on the sheet and put ten dollars into the pot. The winner gets to donate the sum to the charity of his or her choice."

Her excitement mounting, Libby did as ordered, making sure her picks were the opposite of the ones Holden chose.

And Emily was right, she soon found out. Ribbing Holden, and getting teased in return, garnered a great deal of enjoyment.

Unable to stop smiling, she headed to the kitchen between the first and second games.

Holden was pulling out trays of barbecue and all the fixings from Sonny's Barbecue Restaurant.

She marveled at his multitasking hosting skills. "How can I help?"

"Says the woman who whipped my ego in the first game," he told her flippantly.

She came closer and taunted him with an impudent smile. "The day is young, or so they're saying out there."

"They're right." Holden paused. He favored her with a

sexy half smile, his eyes roving her face. "Have I told you how pretty you look today?"

Libby swallowed at the rough note of possession in his voice. He made her feel beautiful whenever he looked at her like that. She met his too-innocent gaze head-on. "You look mighty fine yourself, cowboy."

He grinned wickedly. "Come closer and say that."

Curious, Libby took two steps forward. All the humor left his gaze, replaced by something much more dangerous. She sent him a level look, aware her heart was racing again.

"Holden...your family..."

"I don't care," he whispered ardently, fitting his lips over hers. "I need you. Need this."

And so, it turned out, did Libby. Their days and nights apart—had been excruciatingly lonely.

And that pent-up passion came forth in their kiss.

How long it would have continued, had the wolf whistles and clapping not sounded behind them, Libby would never know.

Flushing, she pulled back. Turned to see that they had quite an audience. The McCabes chorused their approval with huge grins.

"And here we thought you were the least romantic among us," Jeb drawled.

"Clearly, not anymore," Hank ribbed.

Even Shane McCabe, who usually chose not to weigh in on matters of the heart, smiled. "Looks like congratulations of some sort are in order," he declared.

"STOP GLOATING," Holden teased hours later, when the games were over and everyone had left.

Thanks to the use of disposable dinnerware, and the

McCabe habit of pitching in, cleanup was left to a minimum. That mostly consisted of straightening a few throw pillows and carrying the bagged trash out to the cans.

"You beating me every single time was merely a matter of beginner's luck."

"Or," Libby retorted, enjoying the bantering and camaraderie as much as she loved his kisses, "as your brothers put it, your inability to keep your besotted mind 'in the 'game.'"

Holden winked and lifted his hands in a humorous admission of defeat. "I am a little distracted these days."

No kidding. So was she. "Speaking of which," Libby chided, still feeling a little embarrassed at the memory of their recent public display of affection, "you didn't have to kiss me like that in front of your family."

Holden scrubbed a hand over his jaw. "You're right." He leaned toward her, planting a palm on the counter on either side of her and trapping her there. "I shouldn't have kissed you like that." He fitted his body to hers, hardness to softness, until she sighed. "I should have kissed you like this."

The next thing Libby knew she was in his arms. Holden took her lips with a rush of passion, kissing her long and hard and deep. And heaven help them both, she was clinging to him and kissing him back with the same need and intensity.

It had been a mistake thinking she could ever tame or restrict this man with a rebound-romance agreement, Libby thought, when she really had a tiger by the tail.

But maybe it was best this way. To not overthink this. To just feel….

Reveling in the euphoric feelings rushing through her, she let him lift her onto the counter and step between her spread legs. "Now, where were we?" he teased, palming the weight of her breasts through her knit shirt, easily working her nipples to aching peaks. "Oh, yes, we were talking about what kind of kisses are suitable to give you in front of company." He kissed her cheek, her chin, the hollow of her throat. "How about these?"

A shallow breath soughed between her lips. "Good," she murmured back, kissing the strong column of his throat in turn. "All good…"

"How about this?" Holden demonstrated a very potent lip-lock with a lot of heat and pressure.

Libby's heart fluttered in her chest. Body pulsing, straining for more, she wrapped her jean-clad legs around his waist, scooting forward until his arousal pressed against her.

"Very nice, too…" She gasped as he slid his palms beneath her buttocks and pulled her even tighter against him. "But I'm not sure it's the kind of thing that's good for a PDA…."

"You're right." He swept his tongue into her mouth and kissed her so deeply and rapaciously she moaned. Grinning with masculine satisfaction, Holden slowly ended the kiss. His gaze lovingly roved her upturned face. "We should keep this just for us."

Holding her masterfully in his arms, he tugged her off the counter and carried her up the stairs to his bed.

He paused to turn the two battery-driven hurricane lanterns on low, infusing the room with a soft, ultraromantic glow. Then he returned to her side and gave her the kind of nothing-held-back kiss she had been wanting all evening. His mouth moved on hers effortlessly, demandingly, until she was lost in the sweet, wild wonder of his embrace.

Murmuring his name, Libby dragged him closer still,

burying both hands in his hair, opening her mouth to his, every feminine inch of her aroused by his unswerving resolve to possess her. Need swept through her, until her nipples budded and her knees weakened treacherously. They undressed each other and she started to sink onto the bed.

Holden, she soon discovered, had other ideas.

Kissing her all the while, he backed her to the wall and positioned her against it. Once there, he looked down at her with such intensity she almost couldn't breathe.

No longer content just to kiss her, he bent his head and moistened the delicate aureole of her breast. Suckled it gently. Then turned to her other breast, delivering the same patient adoration until she trembled, unsure how much she could take.

"Holden…" How was it possible that someone so big and strong and male could have such a tender touch?

"Let me love you, Libby," he whispered as he replaced his lips with the pads of his thumbs and rose to kiss her again, deeply and erotically, as if she were his and always would be. "The way you were meant to be loved…"

Kneeling in front of her, he gently parted her thighs. Libby closed her eyes and moaned as he found her in the most intimate of caresses. Making lazy circles, moving up, in, out again. Just when she thought she could stand it no more, she quivered with pleasure and catapulted head over heels into bliss….

She'd barely stopped shuddering when he rose and situated himself between her thighs, pausing only long enough to sheathe himself, before kissing her on the mouth, lifting her and parting her, pushing past to the welcoming warmth inside.

They locked eyes and she offered herself to him completely, giving him the kind of access to her heart and soul she had never permitted before.

She knew there were no guarantees in life; the past had taught her that. She knew that the chance to be with Holden like this might be as fleeting as the rebound-romance deal they had initially made with each other.

But if she didn't take advantage of the chance they were being offered, she knew she would regret it for the rest of her life.

Christmas came but once a year.

The chance to be loved like this, and love in return, even less frequently.

This man, this moment, were her holiday gift.

And she didn't intend to squander it.

Wanting to draw out the moment as much as possible, she explored his back and hips and thighs with questing caresses that had him arching in passion.

He surged into her, entering and withdrawing in slow, shallow strokes that soon had her moaning for more.

Trembling with her need, she let every part of her adore every part of him. Rocking against him, with him, urging him on until at last she surrendered to a wild, untamed pleasure unlike anything she had ever known.

HOLDEN MADE LOVE TO LIBBY two more gloriously satisfying times before they finally cuddled together, half-asleep.

"Holden?" she asked softly.

He loved the way she felt, so soft and warm and completely feminine. "Hmm?"

She rose slightly and propped her chin on her hand. Looking delicious ravished, yet heartbreakingly vulnerable, she continued, "You know what you said when Emily was teasing us about us being involved?"

He nodded, recalling the "announcement" to his family.

Libby raked her teeth across her lower lip, her uncertainty apparent. "Why did you make it—us—sound so serious?"

Her question was tentative, testing. Holden sensed one wrong move would have her dashing in the other direction. He could feel how wary she was. How unwilling to be hurt.

Determined not to let her shy away again, he said, "They can all see the same thing we can—that our relationship is likely to extend past the holidays." *Well past, in fact.* "I wanted them to know this was no longer a six-week matchup. That it was more serious than that."

And if he had his way, Holden thought, cuddling Libby close, they would soon be even more serious....

Chapter Fourteen

"Something sure smells good in here," Holden said on Sunday evening.

Someone sure *looked* good, Libby thought as she ushered him inside and took his coat. Instead of the usual jeans and shirt, he wore a pair of wool slacks and a V-necked sweater. His hair was clean and attractively rumpled, his jaw freshly shaved, and he smelled of a woodsy cologne. His handsome face bore the flush of the brisk winter wind.

Grinning in anticipation, Holden closed the distance between them with sensual grace. "My mouth is watering already."

So was hers. But for a much sexier reason than the dinner she had so lovingly prepared.

Forcing herself to concentrate on the hunger of the man in front of her instead of on where she secretly wanted the evening to lead, she took his hands in hers. Her feminine intuition told her this evening could be a turning point for them. Take them out of rebound territory and into the future. So she wanted everything to go perfectly—which, under the current circumstances, could be a problem. Especially if the way to a man's heart really *was* through his stomach. She tilted her head to one side. "You're not just being polite?" she queried uncertainly, enjoying the way his fingers immediately tightened around hers. "You really think dinner smells good?"

Still holding her hands possessively, he gave her a lazy once-over. "Yeah. Amazing, actually. Why?"

Her heart rate picking up another notch, Libby shrugged. "My sense of smell has been a little off since I was sick last week. Same for my sense of taste. Things that normally appeal to me, like coffee with cream, don't. In fact, I haven't had a taste for coffee at all since then." The last time that had happened was during another very difficult time, just under two years ago....

Oblivious to the reason behind her concern, Holden tucked her in the curve of his arm and pressed an affectionate kiss on her temple. "It's probably better for you, not having all that caffeine."

Libby sighed in relief and leaned into the warm, strong curve of his body. "That's one way to look at it."

The other was not something she wanted to even consider. Not when her relationship with Holden was starting to go so very well....

Glad they were finally about to have dinner alone, after days of juggling and rescheduling, Libby led Holden past the temporary "children's library" room toward the rear of the house.

She had taken pains to set the table just right—with festive holiday dinnerware, cranberry-red linens, an intricate holly centerpiece and candles.

A vanilla-cream-filled dark chocolate Yule log chilled in the fridge. A hearty, homemade chicken potpie with a sage biscuit crust was keeping warm in the oven.

It felt pleasantly intimate, having him here this way. As if they were a real couple, and not just having a temporary fling.

"So. How was your day?" Libby went back to rinsing the salad greens, which she'd been in the middle of when the doorbell rang.

"Busy." Holden lounged beside her. "I had a lot to get caught up on at the ranch." He watched her snap the lid on the salad spinner. "How about you?"

She gave the handle a whirl. "I spent most of the afternoon with Miss Rosa and Miss Mim. We targeted another hundred charitable foundations to approach for help."

His gaze tracked her movements as she reached up into a cabinet for the champagne vinegar. She felt his gaze on her breasts and ribs as surely as she would have his touch.

"Any luck with the ones so far?"

Admiring the way he looked in her kitchen, so big and sexy and male, Libby got Dijon mustard from the fridge and shut it with her hip. "We've heard back from only about fifteen of the original one hundred thus far."

He studied her compassionately. "Not good, I'm guessing?"

Trying not to let her frustration bring her down, Libby measured vinegar, mustard, salt and pepper into a bowl. "Apparently, they all have local charities they support." Which was, she told herself realistically, perhaps the way it should be. For who better to know the most deserving, than people who lived and worked in the community?

He moved slightly to the left as she reached for the tool jar. "Even the ones in Dallas and Houston?"

Emily whisked the ingredients together. "Especially those." She paused to flash him a resigned smile. "It seems there are no shortage of worthy nonprofits doing good work, in need of funds to survive."

"You can't get anyone to help you?" he murmured in concern.

"The universal response so far is that this is the Laramie County commissioners' issue. And should be solved by them." Slowly, she whisked in the olive oil. "We've explained that waiting for that to happen will mean the library will likely be closed well over a year."

Holden leaned against the counter, arms folded. "Let me guess. Not their problem."

She affirmed it with a nod. Satisfied the dressing was properly emulsified, she dipped a spoon in and tasted it. Not sure if it was spicy enough, she offered it to him. "What do you think?"

His lips closed over the spoon with sensual reverence. Eyes locked with hers, he savored the taste. "Delicious."

Libby flushed at the husky, intimate timbre of his low tone, and the desirous look in his eyes. She had the feeling he wanted to forgo dinner and take her to bed. Funny thing was, she wanted that, too....

The buzzer went off.

Jerked from her reverie, Libby went to get the potpie from the oven. Holden gave her plenty of room to maneuver as she moved the piping-hot dish to the trivet on the table.

"So what next?" he continued.

Libby mixed the salad and set the bowl on the table.

She had a few ideas brewing. But she was reluctant to disclose them, for fear they wouldn't work out any better than her idea to appeal to all the existing charitable foundations.

Cautiously, she said, "I'm still working on it. But enough about me and my problems." She guided him to a chair, feeling glad he was there. "Let's talk about you."

"YOU'RE NOT GOING TO TELL me where you put it, are you?" Holden drawled three hours later.

Libby laughed, a soft, silky sound. Her sea-green eyes sparkling, she admitted, "I figured you'd have more fun finding the mistletoe than just standing under it."

"Uh-huh." He let his gaze drift over her, liking the way the trendy skirt and coordinating pine-green sweater gloved her slender form. Lower still, he liked what the black tights and the square-heeled shoes did for her show-girl-sexy legs.

Ignoring the fast-building pressure at the front of his slacks, he countered, "Well, it's not anywhere downstairs."

A saucy smile tugging at her lips, she planted her hands on her hips. "Are you sure?"

Holden considered kissing her again—without standing beneath the holiday greenery. Deciding it might be more fun to wait, he shrugged. "Unless you anchored it under the sofa…?"

"No." Coming closer, she regarded him in a deliberately provocative manner. Color flamed in her cheeks. Her breasts rose and fell with every excited breath she took. "It's up high. Tradition, you know."

The only Christmas tradition he was interested in at the moment was kissing her. Long and slow. Deeply and passionately. And every way in between.

He held her eyes and prodded, "High meaning the second floor?"

Libby winked at him. "I guess we'll just have to see."

This was a big deal, Holden knew. Prior to this, the only time she had allowed him to go upstairs with her was when she was sick. But now that the Lowell family photo gallery and a lot of other artifacts had been packed away and put in storage, it felt more like her house. And it looked more like her place, too, with fresh flowers and other feminine touches everywhere.

"You sure you want to do this?" he asked her quietly. "We could go to my ranch." The way they usually did when they wanted to make love.

Libby shook her head, looking happy and relaxed. "I want to be in my house tonight. Playing by my rules. So start searching, cowboy."

Holden liked the mischief in her voice. It was a side of Libby he'd like to see more often. "Okay, then…" he teased back.

He headed up the front staircase, checking every nook and cranny in the high ceiling as he went. Down the hall, to a bedroom he didn't recognize at all. The feminine furniture, the ribbon-bouquet bedding and the flowery, pastel rug on the floor all said Libby.

With satisfaction, Holden noted that she had finally made the changes she should have long before, making this into her life, her house, her domain. Best of all, in front of her bedroom door was a sprig of mistletoe hanging in plain view. He touched the velvet ribbon holding it pinned to the door frame.

"Found one."

Libby leaned against the portal the way a high-school girl leaned against her locker. Hands folded behind her, she tilted her chin up and taunted softly, "Seems like you owe me a kiss."

Grinning wickedly, he positioned her beneath the green leaves and white berries and indulged, until she was arching against him.

Curious to see what would happen next, he released her.

Taking her role as seductress seriously, she said, "Keep going."

Three steps into the bedroom, he found another. Holden kissed her again, the scent of her perfume waltzing through his system. "Mmm." He sifted his hands through the silk of her hair. Dropped his lips to the soft skin of her throat, the hollow of her collarbone. "This is fun."

Libby sighed and wiggled her body sensuously. "You're right," she murmured, enjoying the chase as much as he was. "And keep looking, 'cause there's one more."

Holden glanced in the one direction she was avoiding. "Here it is." Right over her brand-new brass bed with the very sumptuous-looking mattress and linens.

Playfully, she wreathed her arms about his neck and stood on tiptoe to better align their chests and thighs. "Finally," she whispered, every bit the temptress. "We're right where I want to be…."

Right where Holden wanted to be, too.

He planted one hand at the base of her spine, the other at her nape. His mouth covered hers. Daring to put his feelings on the line, he kissed her, and felt her respond with an immediacy that stunned him. He shuddered as her tongue plunged into his mouth, hotly and passionately. With a soft moan, she threaded her fingers through his hair and brought his lips closer still.

Satisfaction roaring through him, he twined his tongue with hers, drinking in the sweet feminine taste of her lips. She trembled as his hands moved to her breasts, and he realized how much he needed her. And how much she needed him, too.

"Holden…"

He slipped his hands beneath her sweater and cupped the soft weight of her breasts. Her nipples tautened in response, and she swayed against him. His need to be close to her as overwhelming as it was inevitable, he continued kissing her, long and hard and deep. Then soft and slow.

Until the world narrowed to just the two of them once again, and he drew her toward the bed.

They undressed each other slowly, kissing and caressing as they went. All layers of restraint fell away, and Holden drew Libby down between the sheets.

Ever so delicately, he traced her curves, delighting in the way her flesh heated beneath his palms. Bending his head, he caressed her creamy breasts and kissed her peach-colored nipples, sucking and caressing them until her hips rose off the bed to meet him.

"Oh, Holden," she whispered, clinging tight, "I want you so much."

"I want you, too, sweetheart." His own body shaking with the effort to contain his desire, he parted her legs, then rubbed and stroked. She caressed him in turn, bringing him to readiness.

"Now," she demanded, pushing him onto his back and climbing astride him. He throbbed against her surrendering softness. The connection turned even more reckless. She drew him in lustily even as he found the soft, sensitive spot with his thumb. And then he was going deeper still, filling her to overflowing, as she rocked against him. She moaned and clung to him, kissing him even as she climaxed. He followed, hard and fast, taking everything she offered and giving her everything in return.

Knowing, if they were as smart as he intended them to be, that it would always be this way. He would be hers. She would be his. And together they'd find a way to have a satisfying future.

But for now, Holden thought, it was enough just to lie here with Libby wrapped in his arms, clinging to him, as if she, too, knew this was the way it was meant to be.

LIBBY HITCHED IN A BREATH, aware that, as always, Holden made her feel so warm and safe. Even when she was trembling and falling apart. And she knew, even if this wasn't the pact they had made, that it was what she wanted. Not just now, but forever. Holden. In her arms. In her bed. Making hers a life worth celebrating to the max.

Knowing that gave her the courage to ask the kind of thing she'd never been brave enough to venture before.

Libby rose up on her elbows.

Affection glowing in his eyes, Holden sifted his fingers through the mussed strands of her hair. "Something on your mind?" he asked quietly.

She nodded. "This isn't the way I had planned to do it, but…" Usually, when it came to relationships, she let the man make all the moves, rather than risk rejection.

But she'd gone after what she wanted just now, in the bedroom, and succeeded. So maybe she could do this, too.

Misunderstanding her hesitation, Holden stroked his hands over her hair and teased, "Sweetheart, we can make love any number of ways…."

Libby chuckled. She knew that, too.

"It's not that," she said.

"Then…?"

She gathered her courage and pushed on. "I want to invite you to the dealership Christmas party next Saturday evening. It's going to be a much bigger fete than usual, and definitely the last one I will ever host. So…"

"You're still feeling a little nervous?" he guessed.

Libby nodded in relief. "Even though I know everyone is pretty much on board with the sale now, there's still a chance the party may not go all that well."

"And that being the case, you'd like a little backup on hand."

Actually, she thought, it was more than that. But not sure how she should say it, she drew in a long breath and continued, "Anyway, I was wondering if you'd be my date for the evening."

He looked deep into her eyes. "Officially?"

"Very officially," Libby affirmed.

A slow, sexy smile crossed his face as he took her hand and lifted it to his lips. "Then it will be my pleasure."

"YOU'RE SURE THAT'S what you want to do with the proceeds from the sale of the dealership?" Claire McCabe said, after Libby had discussed it with her at length on Tuesday.

"Yes." Libby sighed, relieved to finally know what she was going to do with the million dollars she would garner from the sale of the dealership. "As long as it's legally viable, works out taxwise…and we can accomplish it by the end of the year."

"It is. And we can."

Libby gave her attorney a thumbs-up sign. "Then let's go for it," she said, encouraged to find she was no longer confused about what she wanted to do with the rest of her life—professionally, anyway. Personally was another matter….

The paralegal stuck her head in the door, interrupting Libby's musing. "Jeff Johnston and his team are here for the meeting."

Claire held the copies of the contract they were proposing. "Ready?"

Libby nodded.

This was a good thing, she assured herself firmly. The right thing.

For Percy and his family, and for her…

Short minutes later, the two teams were seated opposite one another.

It was a little lopsided. Libby had opted to appear with only her attorney, and the compiled financial data and appraisals. However, Jeff Johnston had brought along the chief financial officer for his entire company, a commercial real-estate broker, a private real-estate broker and two attorneys.

So there were six people on his side of the conference table, two on hers.

Libby immediately saw it for what it was, as did her attorney.

Intimidation.

"Let's get down to business," Claire said, with a brisk, matter-of-fact smile.

Jeff had insisted upon delivering his offer in person. He handed them his written bid.

It didn't take Libby long to spot the glaring omission in Jeff's proposed contract. "There's nothing in here stating the current Lowell Ranch Equipment employees will keep their present salary and position. And nothing at all about the five-percent share in annual company profits you've promised them."

Jeff gestured broadly. "I gave them my word. I'll keep it."

"Then why isn't it in writing?" she demanded.

"If it's part of the proposed acquisition, it has to be spelled out in the contract," Claire insisted.

Libby noted that no one on Jeff's team was surprised by the omission—or her reaction. Which probably meant it wasn't the first time it had happened.

Keeping her composure, she rose. If they wanted to play these games, so be it.

She looked at her attorney. "Clearly, this is not a serious offer. So it's not worth my time or yours."

Her posture militant, Libby headed for the door.

"Now, hold on there a minute," Jeff said. Leisurely, he kicked back in his chair. "We can proceed on a handshake."

"No," Libby said, with as much steel in her voice as there was amiability in his. "We cannot." She glanced at her attorney, leaving no doubt about the strength of her resolve. "And we will not."

"OBVIOUSLY, JOHNSTON LOOKED into my background, too, and decided he could push me around," Libby fumed less than an hour later.

From the meeting, she had gone straight to Holden's ranch, spotting his pickup in one of the fields. Cursing her lack of boots, she had driven out to find him.

He'd stopped repairing fence to get a blanket and spread it on the bed of his truck. Then, hands on her waist, he'd lifted her up so she could sit with her legs dangling over the side.

"You don't look like much of a pushover now," he observed.

Libby tried to tug the skirt of her trim black business suit to her knees, but gave up. Savoring the feel of the winter sun on her shoulders, and the warmer than usual afternoon breeze, she retorted, "That's because I'm not! But two years ago, and long before that, all I cared about was trying to live my life as nonconfrontationally as possible."

Holden went back to the fence he was repairing. "Because you were orphaned," he guessed.

Gazing out across the pasture, Libby reflected, "To be perfectly honest, it probably started way before then."

He pulled the split post out of the ground, then regarded her curiously.

Aware they had never talked about their childhoods, Libby confessed, "My parents were both very single-minded. As an only child, all the emphasis was on me."

Holden, who'd had three siblings, made a face.

Libby sighed and continued, "I learned pretty quickly as a kid that whatever outfit my mother wanted me to wear was the one I was going to put on that day. And the same went for my dad. He expected me to keep my toys and books picked up and put away, just so, and I did," she recollected wearily. "Because if I put my books on a different shelf than the one he had in mind, I was just going to have to do it all over again."

His shirt stretching tight across his shoulders, Holden pounded a new post into the ground. "Doesn't sound like there was a lot of room to negotiate," he observed.

No kidding.

Libby grimaced. "There was even less after they passed, and I went to live with Aunt Ida. She was in her late fifties by then, and had never married or had children. And she liked her life just so." Libby studied the herd of quarter horses grazing in the distance. "It was easier to go along with what she wanted than to fight anything."

Holden pounded in another post. "And Percy, God love him, wanted everything his way, too."

Libby gestured helplessly, recollecting that her husband, too, was an only child. She frowned. "His parents indulged him terribly, trying to keep him happy. Having me cater to his every need only perpetuated that."

Holden stripped off his leather work gloves and strode back to the truck. "But now you're different." He picked up a bottle of water and drank thirstily.

Libby tore her eyes from the strong column of his throat and neck. "You know I am. The last two years have made me think long and hard about who I am and what I want out of life."

Holden wiped the moisture from his lips with the back of his hand. "Do you think Johnston was trying to cheat you?" He offered her the bottle.

Finding she was thirsty, too, Libby took it and drank deeply, before handing it back. "Initially, yes. But since he doesn't have that reputation, I'm more inclined to believe that what went on today was all just a negotiating ploy."

Holden could not disagree with her assessment. "So you're still interested in doing business with him." He hefted himself up to sit beside her on the bed of the truck.

Although she could have shifted over, Libby stayed where she was, letting their hips and thighs touch.

Absorbing the warm masculinity of his body wedged up against hers, she shrugged. "More than ever, oddly enough. Jeff has some great ideas for expanding the business and taking it into the twenty-first-century internet sales and service in a way that, to be perfectly honest, I could never do." She shifted slightly, to better look into Holden's eyes. Her stocking-clad knee nudged his denim-clad thigh in the process.

Swallowing, Libby continued, "Under his guidance, I know the dealership will be a success and continue on in the tradition of excellence that the Lowell family was famous for." She paused briefly to reflect. "It will be a way of keeping Percy and his family alive, even though I'm still planning to move on." *Here, hopefully, with you...*

Holden rested his hand on her knee. "So where do I come into all this?" he said softly, intuiting there was more.

Glad they were on the same page, Libby smiled and looked deep into his eyes. "That's what I wanted to talk to you about."

"LIBBY IS REALLY OUTDOING herself this year, isn't she?" Emily remarked to Holden, one week later, as she parked the Daybreak Café catering van at the rear of the dealership.

He smiled at his sister. "By giving a Christmas party for all her employees and their families...not to mention a few reporters and any and all customers and library patrons who want to attend? I would have to say so."

"I think it's nice that she wants to go out in such a big way. Not that I've seen the two of you together all that much this week."

That, Holden thought, was his one regret. "Libby has been really busy," he said as he helped his sister load desserts onto a cart. "She was in meetings with Jeff Johnston and Claire on Wednesday and Friday."

"She was in Claire's office all day Thursday, too, wasn't she?" Emily brought out plastic-covered trays of appetizers.

Holden nodded. "She had to sign more documents this morning. At the bank and in Claire's office."

"Well, at least financially she should be set when all this is done."

That was true, Holden thought. Libby would have the means to settle wherever she wanted, in style.

"Do you know what her plans are for after the holidays?"

He refused to let his lack of information frustrate him. He knew Libby wanted to make her own decisions and prove she could handle this, all on her own.

He shook his head. "I know she's weighing her options."

Beyond that he had no clue whether she planned on staying in Laramie County, or even if she wanted to continue seeing him.

Although he knew what he wanted. Libby in his life, from here on out.

"What has she said?" his sister probed.

"Not a lot," he admitted reluctantly. "She's afraid she might disrupt the negotiations if she says much of anything before the contracts are all signed."

Emily sighed. "That's understandable, I guess. Especially given how upset the people in Laramie County were about her selling the dealership to begin with."

Holden pushed the cart, warning, "There's still a lot of uncertainty." Everything could explode if the deal Libby had brokered ended up not being all that it was reputed to be.

Emily held the door. "I know. I hear ranchers worrying every day at the café." She paused, her voice lowered in concern. "How is she doing emotionally?"

Aware that his sister was watching him carefully, Holden stated, "Libby's okay." On the surface, anyway. "I can see her getting stronger, more determined to go through with the sale of the Lowell family business and the reorganization of her life, every day."

But at same time he felt that she was definitely keeping something from him. Something personal. He just didn't know what.

I CAN GET THROUGH THIS, Libby told herself firmly as five o'clock—and the start of the Lowell Ranch Equipment Christmas party—approached on Saturday evening.

I am not going to do what I did before, and imagine all

sorts of things to be true just so I won't be alone. I'm fine. Honestly. And that slight indigestion in my gut, and the wobbling in my knees, is nothing more than yet another ridiculous physical reaction to stress....

To prove it, Libby stood and picked up the notes for the speech she was soon to give.

A second later, Holden walked in. Smiling, he shut the door behind him and he closed the distance between them, draping an arm across her shoulders. The warmth of his nearness spurred her heart to beat a little faster, even before he pressed a brief, tender kiss to her temple.

His eyes darkening with possessive intent, he told her in a low voice, "I am going to be so glad when this party is over and I can take you home."

There it was, the trademark McCabe orneriness that Holden employed whenever he felt her spirits needed a boost.

Glad for the diversion from the huge step she was about to take, Libby let her gaze drift over him. "That sounds so great... You just don't know..."

His expression grew tender. "I think I do. I've missed you this week."

"It'll get better soon," she promised, curling into the warmth of his embrace. "We'll have more time for each other."

"I like the sound of that," he murmured, tucking a lock of hair behind her ear.

Just then a rap sounded on door, interrupting the moment. With a sigh, Libby eased out of his arms and stepped away. "Come in."

The door to her office opened and Claire stuck her head in. "Hey, Libby. Holden. Everyone is here. The microphone is set up."

"Thank you. I'll be right there."

The attorney waved in agreement and took off. Libby turned to Holden, all the emotions she had been holding at bay surging to the fore. "When this is all over I will give you a proper thank-you for all you've done for me this week." In addition to moral support and errand running, he had taken over the library hours at her home.

He returned her hug and lifted her hand to his lips. "Just goes to show what a good team we make," he murmured huskily. "Now, go get 'em, tiger."

Feeling newly confident, Libby walked out into the dealership showroom, to take the stage that had been set up.

Gathered around were all the LRE employees, the library staff and many patrons, and many ranchers from the area. She also saw Jeff Johnston and his team, and Claire. But most of all, there was Holden, patiently waiting, believing in her....

Her nervousness dissipating despite the task at hand, Libby took the microphone and thanked everyone for coming. "Before we start the party, I have a few announcements to make. First—it's official. This afternoon, I sold the dealership to Jeff Johnston. Everything Jeff has promised LRE employees—including the five-percent share of annual company profits—is in the sales contract."

A cheer went up.

Libby smiled, glad to see so many happy faces. Knowing the next part was going to be a tougher sell, she forged on. "In exchange for Jeff's generosity, I have agreed to a change in the name of the business. From here on out, the dealership will be known as Jeff Johnston Ranch Equipment."

Silence fell.

No one looked enthused about that.

In fact, just as Libby had expected, a lot of people looked downright ticked off.

She held up a hand to stave off any boos or negative comments, and continued sincerely, "And while I'm happy for Jeff, this makes me sad." She paused, looking audience members in the eye.

"For generations, the Lowell family served this community and served them well. Which is why I have taken the proceeds from this sale and created a charitable foundation in my late husband's name.

"The Lowell Foundation will serve Laramie County and its residents. And my first project, as director and chairman of the foundation, will be to get the Laramie Public Library back up and running, the way it should be."

THE NEXT FEW HOURS WERE filled with tons of questions, even more congratulations and a lot of celebrating. Finally, four hours later, the dealership was empty, except for Libby and Holden.

She returned to her office, where several empty boxes waited.

Looking unbearably sexy in a dark suit and cobalt-blue shirt that brought out the hue of his eyes, Holden undid the knot of his tie. He lounged in the doorway, one shoulder propped against the frame. "So I guess this means you're staying on in Laramie?"

Nodding, Libby slipped out of her high heels. She flexed her aching feet against the plush carpet, working out the kinks. Exhausted, she took off her earrings, too, and set them on her desk. "This last week has given me a lot to think about. I figured I had to leave Laramie, and all the trappings of being Percy's widow, to move on. When the truth is that experience—all the good and bad of it—made me the woman I am today." Pausing, she gazed up at him reflectively. "I can move on, right here. Honor my past, while at the same time pursuing my future, because if there is one thing all this has taught me, it's that Laramie is my home."

Holden came toward her. "What about the house?"

"I'm keeping it—at least for the time being. That was one of my bargaining chips in the marathon negotiation this week. I told Jeff I would lower the overall price on the sale by removing the house. In return, he said he'd put everything he'd promised the employees in writing...." To her consternation, Libby began to feel a little wobbly again.

Gosh, darn it!

Holden's brow furrowed.

Libby steadied herself by putting a hand on the file cabinet, then went to sit on the edge of her desk. "If I... agreed to a name change of the dealership. Which I think was what he was angling for all along."

Holden walked over and sat down next to her. He took her hand in his. "Then why didn't he come out and say it?"

Libby stared down at their linked hands. "Because when we started talking, I wouldn't even consider selling unless we kept the Lowell name on the business. It was only later," she admitted, tightening her suddenly damp fingers in Holden's, "that I realized what the real purpose of this windfall inheritance could be."

Holden nodded, listening, seemingly unable to take his eyes from her face. Although he looked worried now.

Doing her best to hide her symptoms, Libby forged on. "This way, Percy's family will continue to do a lot of good, and they will be remembered always." She paused to acknowledge quietly, "And I'll be able to help a lot of people, too."

Holden searched her face. "You have always been quite the problem-solving crusader."

She smiled and withdrew her trembling fingers from his, discreetly blotting the moisture on her skirt. "And now...I'll have the funds to..." Libby swore as the room tilted sideways. Or at least it seemed to. That darned dizziness again!

"What is going on with you?" Holden demanded in concern, taking her by the shoulders. "You're white as a ghost!"

And that was the last thing Libby heard.

Chapter Fifteen

"This is ridiculous!" Libby argued as Holden escorted her into the Laramie Community Hospital. "I do not need to go to the emergency room."

"It's Saturday night," Holden stated firmly. "You are not waiting until Monday morning to see your family doctor."

Before she could respond, Paige stepped out of an exam room and approached them. "Hey." The scrubs-clad physician and mother of three paused to put down a chart at the nurses' station, then turned back to them. "What's going on?" Her glance swept over them both, taking in the tender, protective way Holden's arm was clamped around Libby's waist. "I heard you were bringing Libby in."

Relieved to have medical help at long last, Holden confided to their mutual friend, "She hasn't been feeling well since she had a virus a couple of weeks ago."

Paige grabbed a new chart and pen. "Is this true?"

Libby waved off the intermittent bouts of nausea and dizziness, combined with the ever-present urge to curl up somewhere and take a nap. "It's just fatigue. And stress."

And a menstrual period that was nearly three weeks late, causing the physical commotion. There was no way she was going to let herself be prey to another hysterical pregnancy, or even the hint of one, Libby thought grimly. It was bad enough she had allowed that kind of melodrama to happen once before. This time, she was doing the rational thing and keeping her suspicions to herself.

Unfortunately, her lack of full disclosure, to either Holden or her best friend, had Paige's radar on full alert.

Her expression concerned, the physician steered them toward an exam room. "Describe the symptoms."

That, Libby really did not want to do. So instead, she stalled and said, "Aren't you a pediatrician?"

Paige flattened a hand against the door and ushered them inside. "It's the holidays. We're shorthanded tonight. At this moment, the internist on call is busy stabilizing a coronary patient. And the other physicians are busy, too. So unless you want to wait until another doctor can be called in…"

Holden lifted his palm. "We're grateful for the help."

Meanwhile, Libby *was* feeling a little wobbly. Actually, she thought, putting a steadying hand on the gurney, make that a *lot* wobbly.

Holden grabbed her by the waist and lifted her onto the bed. Still holding her, he peered at her face. "Are you going to pass out again?"

Paige broke out the smelling salts and waved the aromatic scent beneath Libby's nose. "You fainted?"

Libby jerked back from the hideous smell. "Just a tiny bit," she admitted grumpily.

Not bothering to hide his concern, Holden told Paige, "She scared the heck out of me."

The pretty physician smiled knowingly. "And you are not a guy who scares easily."

He was gallant, though, Libby thought. Sometimes way too gallant for his own good.

"You'd never know that by the way he's been acting

this evening," Libby grumbled, knowing much more of this tender loving care from him and she would be tied to him emotionally—for life.

Paige reached for a clean cotton gown and handed it to her. "We're going to examine you and see what's going on. Do you want him in with you? Or out in the waiting room?"

Libby didn't even have to think about that, as she admitted reluctantly, "In here." Turning to Holden, she tapped the middle of his broad, strong chest. "I want you to hear it firsthand when they tell me this was just exhaustion."

Because she was definitely not pregnant. It didn't matter how much her mind was trying to trick her into believing it was so.

"Get changed. I'll be right back." Paige eased out. The door shut behind her, leaving Libby and Holden alone again.

"Want help getting into that gown?"

Libby felt so shaky and weak she wasn't sure she could manage. However, there was no need to let her handsome companion know that. He'd only use it to torture her with kindness later. "If you must. And stop smiling."

"Can't help it." He playfully tugged on a lock of her hair before helping her off with her sweater. "You're really pretty when you're cranky." He stepped behind her to allow her some modesty while her bra came off and she eased the polka-dot, green-and-white-cotton gown over her shoulders. "And that temper of yours is working to bring the color back into your face." His fingers brushed her skin as he tied the gown in back, then helped her to her feet.

A short time later, she was relaxing beneath the sheet. Holden kept up the chitchat until Paige returned with an E.R. nurse.

Libby answered a ton of questions. Endured a physical exam and gave blood and urine samples.

After an interminable wait, which in reality was only twenty minutes, but was more than enough to tempt Libby to fall asleep, Paige returned.

The auburn-haired physician studied them both, the hint of a smile in her eyes. Finally, she looked at Libby and announced with candor, "The bad news is there's a reason you've been feeling the way you have. And it's likely to continue."

Holden turned and gave Libby an I-told-you-that-you-needed-to-come-in-tonight look.

Paige continued, with a warm smile, "The good news is…you're pregnant."

For a long moment, the mixture of shock and surprise rendered them motionless.

For Libby, this was all too reminiscent of a very similar event—with a very different outcome—two years prior.

She stared at her friend, hardly able to believe… "Are you sure?" she finally gasped, clapping a hand over her heart. "Because we used condoms! Every time!"

Paige smiled.

Holden, Libby noted, couldn't stop grinning like the proud papa-to-be he was.

"No method of contraception is one-hundred-percent fail-safe," Paige said.

"But…" Libby sputtered, still unable to fully comprehend.

"The blood work confirms it. I'm guessing you're due in August. But of course, you'll need to follow up with your ob-gyn." Paige rattled off a few more instructions, then gave Libby a prescription for prenatal vitamins and a list of dos and don'ts for mothers-to-be.

She congratulated them again. Then, leaving them to absorb the news in private, she slipped out of the room.

Holden grabbed Libby and hugged her fiercely. "Can you believe it?" he murmured, every bit as stunned and happy about the news as Libby was, deep down. "We're going to have a baby!"

It was, Libby thought, still struggling with a myriad of emotions, almost too good to be true. For her to suddenly be getting everything she had ever wanted—save love...

"Of course, we'll have to get married right away," Holden stated.

The confidence in his tone snapped her out of her lethargy. "Whoa!" She held up a palm, wishing she had on something other than a hospital gown, which left her feeling far too vulnerable. "You've already had one shotgun wedding," she pointed out, forcing herself to be practical. "You can't do another."

Holden's brow furrowed. "That was different."

Deliberately, Libby ignored the mixture of disappointment and hope on his face: "Yes, you and Heidi had been dating longer than you and I have. And your marriage still failed."

Resentment flashed in his eyes. "*Our* marriage won't fail."

She studied his suddenly poker-faced expression. "Why not?" she demanded impatiently, wishing he could reassure her.

He kept his eyes locked with hers. "Because I care deeply about you and I know you care for me."

Care, Libby thought. Not love...

Unwanted emotion welled up inside her. Wistfulness

and hormones combined, leaving her all the more out of sorts. "Listen to me, Holden." Her temper spiking, Libby folded her arms across her chest. "I know your instincts are noble and that it is very important for you to do the right thing in all situations. But I can't—won't—be a ball and chain to anyone again."

Holden smiled at her in the same indulgent way she had seen other men gaze at their pregnant wives. Gently, he placed his hands on her shoulders. "You wouldn't be a burden to me."

"You say that now," she countered. Doing her best to remain immune to the warmth in his grin, she added, "But as time goes on, you're going to feel cheated. And when that happens—" she swallowed hard, forcing herself to go on "—whatever affection you have for me will diminish."

She held up a hand before he could interrupt. "Maybe only a tiny increment at a time. But it will happen. And then you'll look around and see the kind of deeply loving matches everyone else in your immediate family has made, and you'll regret rushing into this the same way you now regret rushing into that union with Heidi." Tears blurred her eyes. "And I couldn't bear that."

Holden stared at her, his hurt and dismay evident.

Libby mourned, too, but knew the pain he felt now was only a fraction of what he would endure if they continued recklessly down this path.

It didn't matter how she felt, or would always feel, about Holden, Libby thought sternly. It didn't matter that she would marry him in an instant, if only she thought he could love her. She had to do what was right for him. And ultimately, their baby, too. And that meant facing the facts, no matter how harsh.

"I'll share custody of this child with you, and we'll

raise him or her together with all the love and tenderness
we have to give." Hoping to hang on to the passion for as
long as possible she blurted, "And we can even keep the
physical side of our relationship going, as long as it works
for both of us." *As long as you still want me...*

A flicker of interest appeared in his eyes.

"But I won't let you marry me as a point of honor, or
enter into a sham of a marriage, just so everyone else
around us will be happy."

As Holden realized how serious she was, his expression
grew stony. "You're asking us to settle for only a portion
of what we should have."

Feeling as if her whole world were crashing down on
her once again, she edged closer, looked deep into his eyes.
"I'm trying to protect us," she told him softly. "To create
a situation we both can live with."

Holden braced himself as if for battle. "No, Libby," he
argued, "you're *protecting* yourself. And that's not fair to
either of us, never mind our baby!"

"What are you saying?" she whispered, afraid she already knew.

With his jaw clenched, Holden laid down his ultimatum.
"If you don't care enough about me to even consider marriage—after everything we've been through together...
after the incredible way we made love—then it's over,
Libby." He grimaced and stepped back. "It has to be."

"IS THIS A GOOD TIME for us to talk?" Greta asked, several
days later.

It was and it wasn't, Libby thought.

Determined to avoid the subject of her broken heart,
she ushered Holden's mother out of the wintry gloom. The

forecasters were predicting snow, but Libby wasn't expecting that to happen.

She smiled at Greta. "Tomorrow is Christmas Eve. Shouldn't you be getting ready for the big family dinner you're hosting?"

The older woman inched off her leather driving gloves. "I wanted to make sure you were still planning to attend."

There it was, the maternal concern that she so longed to have in her life.

Libby swallowed, figuring she owed it to both of them to be honest. "I didn't think…under the circumstances…" She decided just to come right out with it. "I presume you heard our news?"

Greta smiled, looking overjoyed. "That congratulations are in order? Yes. We do know." She paused to give Libby a warm hug that spoke volumes about the affection and inclusiveness of the McCabe clan. "And we are *so happy* for you and Holden both."

"But—unless I miss my guess—probably not so happy that our rebound romance is officially over."

Looking more thoughtful than upset, Greta allowed, "We're still hopeful things will work out, over time. But that said, the invitation to become a member of the McCabes is still on."

"Because of the baby," Libby stated, needing to know where they all stood.

Greta shook her head. "Because you're you. You're a wonderful young woman, and you need family. And we would love to include you in ours. The same thing goes for your baby, of course."

Libby bit her lip. "Even if Holden and I don't ever marry?"

Greta took her hand and patted it gently. "Our offer is

not conditional. There is no pressure to do anything any one particular way. Love isn't a one-size-fits-all sort of thing."

She continued thoughtfully, "You've seen the different paths it has taken with Holden's siblings and even some of his cousins. Kurt and Paige loathed each other for years before the triplets that were abandoned on his doorstep brought them together."

Libby grinned, recalling, "Hank and Ally came together because of the ranch she inherited."

Greta nodded. "Dylan and Emily tamed each other."

"And Jeb and Cady let a two-week babysitting gig for her sister turn their years-long friendship into something more," Libby recollected.

"And then, of course, there's my beginning with Shane," Greta reminisced fondly. "A late-night mix-up landed us both in the same bed, with our mothers' entire bridge club looking on."

And what a scandal that had been, or so the story went. "The two of you decided the only way to fix it was to get married."

Greta chuckled. "So we eloped to J. P. Randall's Bait and Tackle Shop. And then did everything possible to prove to our matchmaking families that we were not meant for each other."

Creating more legendary scandal in their wake. "And fell in love along the way."

"Very much in love," Greta confirmed, the corners of her eyes crinkling contentedly. "And four children and thirty-six years of marriage later, we're still very much in love."

She leaned forward earnestly. "The point is, we all found love in different ways, and took different paths to get where we are today. So don't feel you have to marry or not marry to get the McCabe stamp of approval, Libby. You already have that." She smiled kindly. "We will love and support you and be there for you no matter what path you-all take. Just make sure whatever path you choose is true to the feelings in your heart."

SHANE MCCABE WALKED INTO the stable and stood looking over the stall door at the foal and mare Holden had just brought in from the pasture. "Is that the Willow I've heard so much about?"

Holden surveyed the breathtakingly beautiful filly with the dark gray mane and tail. "It sure is," he said proudly. He paused to check out the little one's hocks and hooves, gave the filly and her mama a pat, then stepped out of the stall and headed for the tack room to mix up the feed. "She's already got great speed and agility." Which were key traits to an outstanding cutting horse.

Shane nodded in approval. "She's going to make a nice addition to your quarter-horse bloodlines."

Holden thought so, too. His dad stood by while he opened the airtight containers and measured crimped corn, cracked oats and soybean meal into a feed bucket.

Shane handed him the big jar of vitamins, minerals and protein supplements. "Amazing, isn't it," he drawled as Holden added the additional ingredients and a dollop of molasses—for taste—to the feed. "How a mama and a sire that should not have been able to come together and produce a viable heir could not only have done so, but be as happy and thriving as that."

Holden shot his dad a look of muted resentment. "I feel a parable coming on." One relating not to a foal that had survived hemolytic disease, but to him and Libby and the baby they both wanted so very much....

Shane fell into step beside Holden and walked back to the private stall where Willow and her mama were quartered. "Your mother and I know people who did everything 'right.' They followed the prescribed, traditional path of courtship, engagement and marriage, and they still ended up getting divorced."

Holden stepped into the roomy stall and poured mixture into the high and low feeders. "No one in our family really stays on the straight and narrow when it comes to romance, Dad."

Shane watched as he led the filly to the feed mixture. "And you know why that is?"

Holden hunkered down beside Willow as she nosed and nibbled the grains. "I have a feeling you're going to tell me." And it had nothing to do with the fact that Libby did not love him—and apparently never would, Holden thought dispiritedly. Slowly, he got to his feet.

His dad continued, "Because we have all figured out that loyalty to tradition, or really to anything, can take you only so far." Bluntly, Shane stated, "Doing the right thing—the gallant thing—is important."

Holden knew that. He'd been raised on that sentiment.

His dad came closer and clapped a reassuring hand on his shoulder, looking at him man-to-man. "But chivalry is not enough to build a marriage and family on, and never has been. Any more than trading one life for another ensures happiness or parity in the universe."

Heaven help him, Holden thought, biting back an oath. They were talking once again about Percy. About the accident that had claimed him. And Holden's promise to help Percy's widow.

Shane mused soberly, "Fate, destiny, God's will—whatever you want to call it—plays a part in everything that happens and we have no control over that part of our lives, son." He paused, letting his words sink in. "None whatsoever. It's what we do with the hand we are dealt that counts."

THE SNOW STARTED AT two o'clock in the afternoon on Christmas Eve. At first it was just a flake or two, fluttering down from the white sky overhead. Then a light smattering. By four o'clock, it was coming down hard.

Libby gazed out the window, marveling at the miracle and praying it wouldn't be the only one to happen that day. Then she grabbed her coat.

She was just slipping it on when her doorbell rang.

She went to answer it and saw Holden standing there, his hands thrust in his pockets. Snow dusted his Resistol and the shoulders of his shearling-lined suede coat.

Libby wasn't sure what was sexier, the determined look on his handsome face or the fact that he was there at all. She only knew she wanted him in her life. And she hoped—once he heard her out—that he would reconsider and want the same.

She drew a deep, bolstering breath and looked up at him, her heart in her throat and her emotions on the line. "I'm glad you came by."

Silence stretched between them. He stared at her, an undecipherable emotion in his cobalt-blue eyes. "I thought you might like a ride to the gathering at the Circle M tonight."

Although there wasn't a great deal of snow accumulation, the roads were slick. She could see chains on the tires of his all-wheel-drive pickup.

Was that the only reason he was here?

"But," Holden continued in a rusty-sounding voice, still holding her eyes, "before we go…I'd like to talk to you."

Her heart racing, Libby stepped back and ushered him inside.

He took off his coat and hat, and hung them on the coat tree. Libby removed her coat, too, then took him back to the family room, where the Christmas tree had been set up. Too nervous to sit, she turned to face him.

"First, I want to apologize." His expression gentling, he closed the distance between them. "I never should have thrown down that ultimatum." His lips took on a sober slant as he gazed deep into her eyes. "Whatever feels right to you is fine with me."

There was such a thing, Libby realized, as too much latitude in a relationship. She peered at him, struggling to understand. "Does this mean you're taking back your marriage proposal?" Her voice sounded throaty and uneven.

Holden grimaced. "It was more like a marriage *assumption*, but…yes." He caught a lock of her hair and tucked it behind her ear, the gesture so tender it made her want to weep. "I want to wipe the slate clean. It was a thoughtless idea," he confessed huskily, "delivered in a meaningless way." He shook his head regretfully. "I have always thought you deserved better, Libby, and I still do."

Not quite what she had been expecting. But, Libby told herself sternly, it was still a step in the right direction.

She cleared her throat and pushed on with her own much-needed apology. "As long as we're on the subject, Holden, I think you deserve better, too." The longer they stared into each other's eyes, the more her heart thawed. "I haven't been careful with your feelings, or true to what I want in this situation, either."

I haven't been exactly honest. With you or with me.

Holden clasped her hands in his. "If it's more space you need…"

It was time to take the risk, to act based on what was in her heart instead of what would keep her safe. "It's anything but that. The thing is, Holden, I've had a thing for you for quite a while now. I'd like to say it started a month ago, but that would not be true. I was always aware of you, way too aware of you, even back in college when we first met—which was why I had to constantly keep my guard up. The more time I spent with you, the more I liked you." She released a quavering breath. "And I became even more drawn to you after Percy died. You showed me what kind of man you were deep down, and you were so wonderful to me in those few months, so kind and so understanding and tender and caring."

His eyes darkened with emotion. "Since we're being honest here…I felt the same way you did, Libby. And it was not only a forbidden attraction on my part, it was for all the wrong reasons."

Libby nodded, glad he understood. "I knew nothing could come of it because of our mutual guilt. It was like yearning for something you had always wanted and knew deep down was exactly right for you, but never could have." She sighed, remembering. "My hysterical pregnancy and the embarrassing aftermath, our near kiss, was a wake-up call in so many ways, because it all combined to give me the impetus to stay away from you. To get better and wiser and stronger all on my own." Which was something she had needed to do.

"And you have." Holden gave her an admiring glance and brought her all the way into his arms.

Libby splayed her hands across his solid chest and mustered up all the courage she possessed. "And it's because I reached this good place in my life—where I was finally able to separate duty and obligation and people-pleasing tendencies from my need to do what was right for me—that I was finally able to pursue my true feelings for you.

"Of course," Libby continued wryly, feeling the steady beat of his heart beneath her palms, "I went about it all wrong…out of fear of being hurt again."

"Oh, Libby," he whispered hoarsely, planting a kiss on her forehead and waiting for her to continue.

"But—" she gulped, her pulse racing all the more "—maybe because the universe says I am finally due for a little happiness, and because it is Christmas…I ended up where I was supposed to be, just the same. In your life, in your arms…in your bed."

Tears clouding her eyes, Libby took the final leap of faith. "I love you, Holden," she whispered emotionally. "So much."

She wreathed her arms about his neck. Their kiss was long and slow…soft and sweet.

"I love you, too," Holden told her tenderly, then kissed her again even more passionately. Finally he drew back, his resolve as apparent as the depth of his affection. "Enough to do this or not do this in whatever way feels right to you."

From a McCabe man, it was quite an admission. "So," Libby clarified, her heart taking on a happy, excited rhythm, "if I said I never wanted to ever get married again…"

Holden's gaze was steady and sincere. "I would stand by you," he promised.

Delight bubbling up inside her, she said, "But what if I said I wanted to get married—so our baby would be born legitimate—yet not live together?"

He remained unruffled. "I'd be okay with that, too."

Libby looked deep into the eyes of her strong McCabe man and took another deep, bolstering breath. "And if I said I know there will be those who won't approve, and who think you rushed me into bed. Or that I seduced you. And others who assume we are only together because of some outdated notion of shotgun marriage…"

He raised a brow, but patiently heard her out.

She paused to take a last innervating breath. "And yet, what if I say I don't give a hoot what anyone thinks. That I want to marry you anyway. Right here. Right now. *Today.*"

Joy radiated from every fiber of his being. He hugged her close and gave her the confirmation she had been waiting for all her life. "I'd be okay with that, too."

THANKS TO THE WINTRY weather, the drive to J. P. Randall's Bait and Tackle Shop took an hour and fifteen minutes instead of the forty-five Holden had estimated. But Libby didn't mind. It was Christmas Eve. She was pregnant with Holden's baby. He had asked her to marry him, and she had said yes. Life didn't get any better than this. At least that's what she'd thought until they turned into the single-pump gas station.

The squat, flat-roofed building with the peeling white paint was out in the middle of nowhere. Just run-down enough to make it disreputable, not dangerous. Libby'd heard of this place—it was, after all, the stuff of McCabe legends. But she'd never actually been here. "Are you sure this is a wedding chapel?" she asked in bemusement. "'Cause it sure doesn't look like one!"

Holden grinned, looking handsomer than ever as he came around to help her down from the cab. "Positive." They swept through the falling snow to the front of the building. "Says so right here." He pointed to the sign next to the door. "'Bait, fresh and frozen, for sale. Tackle, all kinds. Groceries, beer, coolers and ice available.'"

"'Hunting knives sharpened. Spare tires repaired,'" Libby read, impressed. "'Marriage licenses issued, ceremonies performed.'"

The only problem was a closed sign on the door. Shivering in the cold, Libby rested her back against Holden's chest and leaned into the warm, comforting circle of his arms. "I hope someone is here," she said.

"It would be disappointing as heck to drive all the way out here, wedding rings in hand, only to discover…"

"One way to find out." Grinning, Holden let go of her long enough to pound on the door. And then again.

Finally, fluorescent lights switched on in the store. The door opened. A young man in jeans and a Brad Paisley T-shirt beckoned them on in.

"J.P. Jr.!" Holden greeted him with a warm handshake and a slap on the back.

"Howdy, Holden." The young cowpoke with the spiked haircut and tattoos rocked back on his heels. "What brings you out this way?"

Holden grinned, looking every bit as excited and happy as Libby felt. "We need a marriage license—and a ceremony."

"Following in the folks' footsteps, huh?" J.P. Jr. teased, getting out the paperwork and a tray of rings.

There was something special, Libby thought, about eloping to the same place Greta and Shane McCabe had. It seemed like a good omen for their future.

Holden took Libby's hand securely in his and winked. "Or making our own."

Epilogue

One year later...

Libby had just taken the pecan and cranberry-apple pies out of the oven when Holden appeared in the doorway of the kitchen, three-month-old Cooper cradled in his arms. It was a sight that never failed to warm her heart.

Their son had his daddy's blue eyes and her honey-blond hair. And a quick cherubic smile that could have lit up all of Texas.

As usual, Libby noted fondly, both of the men in her life looked as happy as could be. As was she.

Under her direction, the Lowell Foundation was doing great things all over Laramie County and serving as a coordinating agency for other local charities. The tractor dealership was thriving and the public library was open again. And life as one of the McCabes was better than she ever imagined.

It had been a magical year, and she knew her future with Holden and Cooper and the rest of her new family would only get better.

"You can come and look now," Holden told her. "Coop and I are done putting the finishing touches on the holiday decor."

Contentment flowing through her, Libby walked over to give them each a kiss. "I can't wait to see."

Holden handed her their son for a cuddle, and wrapped his arm around her shoulders. Together, they walked into the family room.

The eight-foot-tall eldarica pine was topped with a shining gold star and threaded with shimmering white lights. The branches were adorned with a wide-ranging selection of ornaments. UT sports, *Sesame Street* characters and the beloved *Peanuts* gang hung next to all the whimsical, one-of-a-kind decorations Libby had picked out the previous year.

Stockings with their names embroidered on them hung on the mantel.

Beneath the tree were presents waiting to be opened.

Mistletoe they had picked themselves was hung strategically throughout the house.

Holden grinned. "Is this a great family Christmas or what?"

"It's spectacular," Libby admitted. "Especially the tree. It beats the his and hers versions we had last year hands down."

"That's what I was thinking. The question is," Holden murmured with another adoring look at her and their son, "what is Cooper thinking?"

Libby looked down at the infant snuggled into the warmth of her breasts. His head was turned slightly to the side, and his eyes were shut in peaceful repose. Soft, rhythmic breath soughed out of his Cupid's bow lips.

Parental tenderness swept through her. "Not much, apparently. Looks like he's just fallen asleep."

Gently, Holden touched the baby's cheek. Then hers.

"What do you think?" he whispered. "Should we put him down?"

Libby nodded in agreement. "It's probably a good idea for him to have as much of a nap as he can get. He's going to need his energy for the Christmas Eve dinner this evening, at your parents' ranch."

They took him up to his crib, covered him with a soft blue blanket and turned on the monitor. Then they tiptoed back out again, and adjourned to their bedroom for a little quiet time of their own.

Holden stopped her beneath the mistletoe. "Have I told you how much I love you?"

"Many, many times." Libby grinned and wound her arms about his neck. "But that's okay." She kissed him passionately. "Because I never get tired of hearing it, and I love you, too, Holden. So much."

He kissed her back.

When at last they drew apart, he looked deep into her eyes and said, "It's time I showed you, too."

He withdrew a velvet gift box from his dresser drawer.

Libby undid the ribbon and opened it up. Inside was a beautiful diamond solitaire, which he slid onto her finger. "It's the engagement ring you never got. The one you would have had if we hadn't eloped…."

Libby couldn't think of a better present. "Oh, Holden," she breathed in delight. "It's beautiful! I love it!" Beaming, she said, "And I have something for you, too!"

She went to her dresser and brought out another small box. Inside was a note that said simply: "IOU a baby girl."

"So whenever you're ready, too, we can get started working on that," she teased, having learned that time was the most precious commodity of all. And never to be squandered. "Or even have a practice run…" Because she and Holden were never ones to put off until tomorrow what could be accomplished today.

"I like the idea of that as much as I enjoyed eloping with you. So…" Holden brought her intimately close, all the love she had yearned for reflected in his eyes. "How about right now, Mrs. McCabe?"

Libby smiled. "Sounds good to me, Mr. McCabe."

And together they went about doing just that.

* * * * *

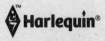

COMING NEXT MONTH

Available November 8, 2011

#1377 A TEXAS RANGER'S CHRISTMAS
American Romance's Men of the West
Rebecca Winters

#1378 HOLIDAY IN A STETSON
Marie Ferrarella and Tina Leonard

#1379 MY CHRISTMAS COWBOY
Men of Red River
Shelley Galloway

#1380 THE CHRISTMAS SECRET
Fatherhood
Lee McKenzie

You can find more information on upcoming
Harlequin® titles, free excerpts and more at
www.HarlequinInsideRomance.com.

HARCNM1011

REQUEST YOUR FREE BOOKS!
2 FREE NOVELS PLUS 2 FREE GIFTS!

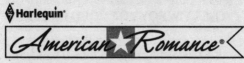

♦ Harlequin®

American ★ Romance®

LOVE, HOME & HAPPINESS

YES! Please send me 2 FREE Harlequin® American Romance® novels and my 2 FREE gifts (gifts are worth about $10). After receiving them, if I don't wish to receive any more books, I can return the shipping statement marked "cancel." If I don't cancel, I will receive 4 brand-new novels every month and be billed just $4.49 per book in the U.S. or $5.24 per book in Canada. That's a saving of at least 14% off the cover price! It's quite a bargain! Shipping and handling is just 50¢ per book in the U.S. and 75¢ per book in Canada.* I understand that accepting the 2 free books and gifts places me under no obligation to buy anything. I can always return a shipment and cancel at any time. Even if I never buy another book, the two free books and gifts are mine to keep forever.

154/354 HDN FEP2

Name	(PLEASE PRINT)	

Address		Apt. #

City	State/Prov.	Zip/Postal Code

Signature (if under 18, a parent or guardian must sign)

Mail to the **Reader Service:**
IN U.S.A.: P.O. Box 1867, Buffalo, NY 14240-1867
IN CANADA: P.O. Box 609, Fort Erie, Ontario L2A 5X3

Not valid for current subscribers to Harlequin American Romance books.

Want to try two free books from another line?
Call 1-800-873-8635 or visit www.ReaderService.com.

* Terms and prices subject to change without notice. Prices do not include applicable taxes. Sales tax applicable in N.Y. Canadian residents will be charged applicable taxes. Offer not valid in Quebec. This offer is limited to one order per household. All orders subject to credit approval. Credit or debit balances in a customer's account(s) may be offset by any other outstanding balance owed by or to the customer. Please allow 4 to 6 weeks for delivery. Offer available while quantities last.

Your Privacy—The Reader Service is committed to protecting your privacy. Our Privacy Policy is available online at www.ReaderService.com or upon request from the Reader Service.

We make a portion of our mailing list available to reputable third parties that offer products we believe may interest you. If you prefer that we not exchange your name with third parties, or if you wish to clarify or modify your communication preferences, please visit us at www.ReaderService.com/consumerschoice or write to us at Reader Service Preference Service, P.O. Box 9062, Buffalo, NY 14269. Include your complete name and address.

HARI1B

Harlequin® Special Edition® is thrilled to present a new installment in USA TODAY *bestselling author RaeAnne Thayne's reader-favorite miniseries,* THE COWBOYS OF COLD CREEK.

Join the excitement as we meet the Bowmans—four siblings who lost their parents but keep family ties alive in Pine Gulch. First up is Trace. Only two things get under this rugged lawman's skin: beautiful women and secrets. And in Rebecca Parsons, he finds both!

Read on for a sneak peek of CHRISTMAS IN COLD CREEK. *Available November 2011 from Harlequin® Special Edition®.*

On impulse, he unfolded himself from the bar stool. "Need a hand?"

"Thank you! I…" She lifted her gaze from the floor to his jeans and then raised her eyes. When she identified him her hazel eyes turned from grateful to unfriendly and cold, as if he'd somehow thrown the broken glasses at her head.

He also thought he saw a glimmer of panic in those interesting depths, which instantly stirred his curiosity like cream swirling through coffee.

"I've got it, Officer. Thank you." Her voice was several degrees colder than the whirl of sleet outside the windows.

Despite her protests, he knelt down beside her and began to pick up shards of broken glass. "No problem. Those trays can be slippery."

This close, he picked up the scent of her, something fresh and flowery that made him think of a mountain meadow on a July afternoon. She had a soft, lush mouth and for one brief, insane moment, he wanted to push aside that stray lock of hair slipping from her ponytail and taste her. Apparently he needed to spend a lot less time working and a great deal *more* time recreating with the opposite sex if he could have sudden random fantasies about a woman he wasn't even inclined to like, pretty or not.

"I'm Trace Bowman. You must be new in town."

She didn't answer immediately and he could almost see the wheels turning in her head. Why the hesitancy? And why that little hint of unease he could see clouding the edge of her gaze? His presence was obviously making her uncomfortable and Trace couldn't help wondering why.

"Yes. We've been here a few weeks."

"Well, I'm just up the road about four lots, in the white house with the cedar shake roof, if you or your daughter need anything." He smiled at her as he picked up the last shard of glass and set it on her tray.

Definitely a story there, he thought as she hurried away. He just might need to dig a little into her background to find out why someone with fine clothes and nice jewelry, and who so obviously didn't have experience as a waitress, would be here slinging hash at The Gulch. Was she running away from someone? A bad marriage?

So…Rebecca Parsons. Not Becky. An intriguing woman. It had been a long time since one of those had crossed his path here in Pine Gulch.

Trace won't rest until he finds out Rebecca's secret, but will he still have that same attraction to her once he does? Find out in CHRISTMAS IN COLD CREEK. Available November 2011 from Harlequin® Special Edition®.

Discover two classic tales of romance in one
incredible volume from

USA TODAY Bestselling Author

Catherine Mann

Two powerful, passionate men
are determined to win back the women
who haunt their dreams…but it will
take more than just seduction
to convince them that this love will last.

IRRESISTIBLY HIS

Available October 25, 2011.